Rokuro-Kubi

Ghost Stories and Strange Tales of Old Japan

LAFCADIO HEARN

With an Introduction by
Oscar Lewis

Illustrated by
Yasumasa Fujita

DOVER PUBLICATIONS, INC.
Mineola, New York

Copyright

Bibliographical Note

This Dover edition, first published in 2006, is a republication of all the illustrations from the work originally published in 1932 by The Shimbi Shoin, Ltd., Tokyo, for the Limited Editions Club, under the title *Kwaidan: Stories and Studies of Strange Things*. The text is from the 1968 Dover edition of the same title. While the first illustration from 1932 edition has been reproduced in color for the front cover, the remaining illustrations that were originally in color are rendered here in black and white. (The first edition of the work was published in 1904 by Houghton, Mifflin and Company, Boston and New York.)

Library of Congress Cataloging-in-Publication Data

Hearn, Lafcadio, 1850–1904.
Kwaidan : ghost stories and strange tales of old Japan / Lafcadio Hearn ; with an introduction by Oscar Lewis ; illustrated by Yasumasa Fujita.
p. cm.
" ... a republication of all the illustrations from the work originally published in 1932 as 'Kwaidan: stories and studies of strange things' by The Shimbi Shoin, Ltd., Tokyo ... The text is from the 1968 Dover edition. The illustrations from the 1932 edition ... originally appeared in color ... [but] are rendered here in black and white"—T.p. verso.
ISBN 0-486-45094-5 (pbk.)
I. Lewis, Oscar. II. Fujita, Yasumasa. III. Title. IV. Title: Ghost stories and strange tales of old Japan.

PS1917.K8 2006
813'.4—dc22

2006046281

Manufactured in the United States of America
Dover Publications, Inc., 31 East 2nd Street, Mineola, N.Y. 11501

Introduction

Soon after Hearn's death in 1904, his Japanese widow made a list of some of the things he had "liked extremely". It is a curious list, yet a revealing one: sunsets, the west, summer, the sea and swimming, banana trees, the Japanese cedar, Martinique, folk songs, *Kwaidan* (ghostly tales), beefsteak, insects, and lonely cemeteries. He also liked plum pudding, hot rooms, tobacco, primitive and naive people, and Herbert Spencer. A catalogue of the things he heartily disliked would be even longer. Mrs. Hearn named only a few: liars, abuse of the weak, Prince Albert coats, stiff shirts, and New York City. The list should be extended, for he very definitely disliked whole sections of Western civilization and, in particular, Western industrialism: noise, machinery, crowds, smoke and dust, hustlers, braggarts, and practically everyone with whom he was forced to have business relations. Hearn was shy, restless, opinionated, quick-tempered, loyal, and morbidly sensitive. He had no talent for adapting himself to uncongenial surroundings, and much of his life was spent in passionate rebellion against the obstacles and irritations that men of milder temperament learn to endure and eventually to ignore. He died at fifty-four and left behind him a few loyal friends, a somewhat longer list of bitter enemies, and a dozen books of such quality as to assure him a permanent place in English literature.

Hearn seldom lived according to rule and he almost never did the expected. His career, like his personality, was picturesque in the extreme. He was born, June 27, 1850, at Santa Maura, an island off the coast of Greece. His father was an Irishman, a surgeon in the British Army, his mother a young Greek woman who was said to be of great beauty and who was unquestionably possessed of an extremely restless spirit. Lafcadio believed, probably with a great deal of truth, that he had inherited all his characteristics from his mother, none from his father. When he was six, the family moved to Dublin, his parents quarrelled and his mother eloped with a native of her own country and was not heard of again. The father presently remarried and Lafcadio was sent to live with a wealthy and highly eccentric great-aunt. A few years later he was sent to Ushaw, a Catholic school at Durham (his picturesque great-aunt having recently been converted to Romanism), where in later years he was remembered equally for his brilliance in English and his contempt for all authority. While he was at play there one day, another boy swung a rope and the loose end struck him in the eye, damaging it so badly that the sight was permanently destroyed. He was already near-sighted, and the subsequent added strain so weakened the other eye that during the remainder of his life Hearn was harried by the fear of total blindness. At seventeen he cut off all connection with his curious guardian and went to London, where he spent two years in such misery and poverty that in after life he almost never referred to this period.

Before he was twenty he came (or was sent) to America, making his way to Cincinnati, where he was to receive an allowance from some connection of his family. The allowance failed to materialize and the destitute youth repeated in the Ohio river town his experience in the London slums. For a time he found shelter in an abandoned boiler in a vacant lot; later an elderly countryman, Henry Watkin, allowed him to sleep on a pile of paper in the rear of his printing shop; later still he was able to afford the luxury of a bed in a dingy rooming-house. He remained in Cincinnati eight years; it was probably the most important period of his life. There the shy, resentful, half-blind little wanderer first learned that he could do certain things better than other men and that, because of his talent, he could force the world to give him a livelihood and a certain amount of half-grudging recognition. Soon after his arrival he had begun to picture himself as an author. One evening he so far mastered his shyness as to force a few pages of manuscript into the hand of an editor of one of the local newspapers. His contribution was printed and he tried again. Presently he was given a table and chair in a corner of the editor's office. Within a few weeks he had become a fixture: a shabby, unprepossessing individual who came and went as furtively as a shadow, and who sat hunched over his paper for hours at a time, writing with enormous concentration.

Within a year he was a star reporter, recognized as the best in his line in the city. His line was a curious one. He wrote atmospheric accounts of events in which violence or horror predominated. More skillfully than any other local writer he catered to the public's taste for grisly details of accidents, murders, violence of all kinds. He wrote an account of a particularly atrocious murder in which the victim's body had been partially destroyed in a factory furnace, conveying the horror of the scene so graphically that his story made a state-wide sensation. For some years Hearn deliberately cultivated this ghoulish form of writing, though as he grew more mature he was able to look back on the laboriously piled-up horrors of this period as an indiscretion of his literary youth.

In Cincinnati he gained confidence in his ability, made a few congenial friendships among other newspapermen, did much reading and writing and, outside office hours, lived a curious life of which his friends had only occasional glimpses. Hearn held no exalted opinion of the conventions of the time and place. His life-long interest in the strange and bizarre, in the curious customs and legends of alien races—the same interest that more than twenty years later was to produce *Kwaidan*—had already manifested itself in the Ohio town in the middle '70s. He found a strange fascination in the life of the negro colony along the riverbank, and haunted its saloons and dives, studying its half-primitive inhabitants at their work and play, listening to their songs and music, witnessing their dances and brawls and quite naive carnalities. It was an interest shared by few of the respectable white element of Cincinnati. Presently it began to be said of Hearn that in his private life he associated exclusively with negroes, and the scornful little Irishman was by no means careful to avoid giving some point of truth to the rumor. This circumstance, combined with a longing for the warmth and color of a milder climate, at length brought the Cincinnati period to a close and he set off, in 1887, for New Orleans.

So far as Hearn's literary development is concerned, it may be said that he served his apprenticeship in Cincinnati and that during the New Orleans period he learned how to apply his talent, acquiring the mental training and finish of style that made possible the enduring quality of the books he was to write in Japan. His stay in New Orleans lasted ten years. He had entered the city unknown; when he left, his reputation as an accomplished journalist had spread throughout the South and his contributions to Eastern magazines had given him the beginnings of a national reputation. The latter part of this New Orleans period seems to have been the only time in his life when he was entirely content for more than a few months at a time. His newspaper work, after he joined the staff of the *Times-Democrat* in 1881, was congenial; he was a "special writer" with ample freedom to pursue his enthusiasm for the weird and curious in literature. He did translations from the exotic French writers of his own and earlier periods, searched the literatures of the Orient for odd legends and bizarre fragments, which with much pains he put into English that had all the richness and color of the originals.

In New Orleans, too, he found an environment more nearly to his liking than any he had yet encountered. All his life Hearn took a feline delight in physical warmth and he toiled through the sweltering New Orleans summers with complete content. It was the city's nearness to the tropics that eventually caused him to leave. The warm winds blowing in over the Gulf, the markets piled high with tropical fruits, the native crews of the little trading ships from the south, all filled him with a desire to experience the real thing. Eventually the wish became too strong to resist; he left New Orleans, spent a month in New York—a city for which he held a most distinguished dislike—and in March, 1887 sailed for the West Indies. For a time the tropics more than fulfilled his expectations. His letters from Martinique radiate the confidence and content of a man who has found what he wants and for whom life presents no further problems. But Hearn's was not the sort of life to be long free from problems. Adversity had a way of descending upon him when he felt most secure; moreover his temperament was such as to render prolonged periods of tranquillity altogether impossible.

He had been in his island Eden only a few months when he was beset by half a dozen forms of trouble: sickness, a climate that for once was too hot for sustained work, failure to receive prompt payment for the magazine articles he sent north, and the conviction—always a common one with Hearn—that he was being persecuted and cheated by the men who published his work. However, the Martinique period resulted in the publication of his first important book, *Two Years in the French West Indies,* and added considerably to his growing reputation. It added very little, however, to his never well-filled purse, and Hearn spent an unhappy few months in Philadelphia and New York trying with indifferent success to play the role of magazine free-lance and minor literary celebrity. Only pride and a stubborn refusal to acknowledge defeat prevented his returning to the security of his berth on the New Orleans newspaper. It is curious to know that when the suggestion was made that he go to Japan and write a series of studies similar to those contained in his Martinique book, Hearn at first viewed the project without enthusiasm. He doubted his ability to understand and interpret the Japanese, so vastly more complex than the naive children of the tropics. He was certain that it would take years of observation and study before he could presume to write a book on Japan. Moreover, it involved traveling half around the world, with the prospect of finding himself stranded in a completely alien land. Nevertheless, he set off, in the winter of 1890, on what he thought would be a journalistic tour that might last two or three years at the most. It lasted fourteen years and was terminated only by his death.

Almost from the moment he set foot on the island, Hearn realized his stay was to be a long one. With characteristic lack of prudence he had, soon after he arrived, severed his connection with the magazine that was to publish his studies. Almost without funds, in a strange land where he was entirely unknown, Hearn was yet able to forget the uncertainty of his own prospects in his delight at the curious new world into which he had been projected. To Joseph Tunison, friend of his Cincinnati days, he wrote less than a month after his arrival:

> "The country is . . . full of the strangest charm. Artistically it is one vast museum. Socially and naturally it is really Fairyland. The first impression produced by the Japanese themselves is that of being among the kindest kind of fairies . . . The religions seized my emotions at once, and absorbed them. I am steeped in Buddhism, a Buddhism totally unlike that of books—something infinitely tender, touching, naif, beautiful. I mingle with the crowds of pilgrims to the great shrines; I ring the great bells; and burn incense-rods before the great smiling gods."

For the remaining fourteen years of his life Hearn continued both figuratively and literally to burn incense-rods before the smiling gods of old Japan. He early realized that the country presented an amazingly fertile field for the exercise of his peculiar variety of talent. For it was in the study of alien beliefs and customs and in the interpretation of an alien environment and viewpoint that Hearn found his chief interest. He was quite content to let others write travel books or concern themselves with the politics or economics or formal history of a country. For himself he preferred a far smaller canvas, one which he could fill in slowly, patiently, with such a wealth of carefully selected detail that when he had finished he had projected for his readers, compactly yet with perfect clearness, some minor but significant phase of the daily life of a people, some illuminating sidelight on the native literature or religion, some quaint bit of folklore. In Japan Hearn found for the first time an inexhaustible store of such literary material, and he continued to draw on it with undiminished industry and zeal as long as he lived. Naturally, it was not long before his particularly effective method of interpreting a nation had begun to attract the attention of readers. Hearn's first book on Japan appeared four years after he arrived, in 1894. It found a small but appreciative audience; an audience that grew slowly but inevitably as each of the eleven titles published during his lifetime came from the press. Although his books never sold sufficiently well to assure financial security for himself and his family, he yet lived long enough to enjoy the praise of discriminating minds both in America and England and to see the beginnings of a reputation that promised to outlive him by many years.

The outlines of his life in Japan are well known. After a few months, he managed to be appointed a teacher in a native school in the province of Izumo, where he spent several productive years and where, having determined to spend the rest of his life in Japan, he married a young Japanese woman of ancient Samurai lineage. From Izumo he went as a teacher in the High School at Kumamoto. After several years he was appointed a professor of English literature in the Imperial University at Tokyo, where he laid the foundations for a reputation as a teacher of remarkable inspirational quality; a reputation which his former students have delighted to keep alive to this day. During most of his stay in Japan, hence, Hearn devoted his talents and energy to a double task. In the classroom he labored to instil into his Japanese students an understanding of the history and traditions of English literature and an appreciation of its masterpieces, and in his study at home he toiled patiently for hours each day interpreting for Western readers the simplicity and beauty of those phases of Japanese life that he found prepetually fascinating. That he was able to carry out this two-fold mission with so much skill and in spite of the most discouraging of handicaps—ill health, the never distant threat of blindness, politics within the Japanese school system which eventually cost him his teaching position, and a miserably small financial return from his books—is tribute alike to the man's courage and to his intellectual stature.

Kwaidan was next to the last book Hearn wrote, and the last that he actually saw in the completed state. It was published in April, 1904 and its author died five months later, on September 16, while his *Japan: An Attempt at Interpretation* was going through the presses. Hearn had been living in Japan more than a dozen years when *Kwaidan* was written, and inevitably some of his early enthusiasm for the country had been tempered by increased familiarity and more accurate understanding. But for the rich and varied folklore of the Japanese Hearn's admiration had by no means slackened. To the last, he was as eager to unearth some quaint legend or trace down some curious bit of superstition as he had been during the first months after his arrival, and he worked with the same slow patience to render his discoveries accurately and without distortion into English. After he died, his widow wrote of some of his struggles to put into another tongue the exact feeling and atmosphere of these "ghostly tales" of old Japan; how he made her enact again and again a part in some ancient legend, studying her every gesture, insisting on the exact intonation of every word. "Had anyone seen us from the outside," she adds, "we must have appeared like two mad people." Readers of the following pages will not regret Hearn's passion for accuracy in detail and atmosphere, for here we have a group of tales of ancient Japan rendered with a fidelity to the originals that can be found nowhere else in the English language.

OSCAR LEWIS

Contents

Preface

Most of the following *Kwaidan,* or Weird Tales, have been taken from old Japanese books—such as the *Yasō-Kidan, Bukkyō-Hayakkwa-Zenshō, Kokon Chomonshū, Tama-Sudaré,* and *Hyaku-Monogatari.* Some of the stories may have had a Chinese origin: the very remarkable "Dream of Akinosuké", for example, is certainly from a Chinese source. But the Japanese story-teller, in every case, has so recolored and reshaped his borrowing as to naturalize it. . . . One queer tale, "Yuki-Onna", was told me by a farmer of Chōfu, Nishitamagōri, in Musashi province, as a legend of his native village. Whether it has ever been written in Japanese I do not know; but the extraordinary belief which it records used certainly do exist in most parts of Japan, and in many curious forms. . . . The incident of "Riki-Baka" was a personal experience; and I wrote it down almost exactly as it happened, changing only a family name mentioned by the Japanese narrator.

L.H.

Tōkyō, Japan, January 20, 1904.

KWAIDAN

The Story of Mimi-Nashi-Hōïchi

The Story of Mimi-Nashi-Hōïchi

More than seven hundred years ago, at Dan-no-ura, in the Straits of Shimonoséki, was fought the last battle of the long contest between the Heiké, or Taira clan, and the Genji, or Minamoto clan. There the Heiké perished utterly, with their women and children, and their infant emperor likewise—now remembered as Antoku Tennō. And that sea and shore have been haunted for seven hundred years. . . . Elsewhere I told you about the strange crabs found there, called Heiké crabs, which have human faces on their backs, and are said to be the spirits of Heiké warriors.[1] But there are many strange things to be seen and heard along that coast. On dark nights thousands of ghostly fires hover about the beach, or flit above the waves—pale lights which the fishermen call *Oni-bi,* or demon-fires; and, whenever the winds are up, a sound of great shouting comes from that sea, like a clamor of battle.

In former years the Heiké were much more restless than they now are. They would rise about ships passing in the night, and try to sink them; and at all times they would watch for swimmers, to pull them down. It was in order to appease those dead that the Buddhist temple, Amidaji, was built at Akamagaséki.[2] A cemetery also was made close by, near the beach; and within it were set up monuments inscribed with the names of the drowned emperor and of his great vassals; and Buddhist

[1] See my *Kottō,* for a description of these curious crabs.

[2] Or, Shimonoséki. The town is also known by the name of Bakkan.

services were regularly performed there on behalf of the spirits of them. After the temple had been built, and the tombs erected, the Heiké gave less trouble than before; but they continued to do queer things at intervals—proving that they had not found the perfect peace.

Some centuries ago there lived at Akamagaséki a blind man named Hōïchi, who was famed for his skill in recitation and in playing upon the *biwa*.[1] From childhood he had been trained to recite and to play; and while yet a lad he had surpassed his teachers. As a professional *biwa-hōshi* he became famous chiefly by his recitations of the history of the Heiké and the Genji; and and it is said that when he sang the song of the battle of Dan-no-ura "even the goblins [*kijin*] could not refrain from tears".

At the outset of his career, Hōïchi was very poor; but he found a good friend to help him. The priest of the Amidaji was fond of poetry and music; and he often invited Hōïchi to the temple, to play and recite. Afterwards, being much impressed by the wonderful skill of the lad, the priest proposed that Hōïchi should make the temple his home; and this offer was gratefully accepted. Hōïchi was given a room in the temple building; and, in return for food and lodging, he was required only to gratify the priest with a musical performance on certain evenings when otherwise disengaged.

One summer night the priest was called away to perform a Buddhist service at the house of a dead parishioner; and he went there with his acolyte, leaving Hōïchi alone in the temple. It was a hot night; and the blind man sought to cool himself on the veranda before his sleeping-room. The veranda overlooked a small garden in the rear of the Amidaji. There Hōïchi waited

[1] The *biwa*, a kind of four-stringed lute, is chiefly used in musical recitative. Formerly the professional minstrels who recited the *Heiké-Monogatari*, and other tragical histories, were called *biwa-hóshi*, or "lute-priests". The origin of this appellation is not clear; but it is possible that it may have been suggested by the fact that "lute-priests", as well as blind shampooers, had their heads shaven, like Buddhist priests. The *biwa* is played with a kind of plectrum, called *bachi*, usually māde of horn.

for the priest's return, and tried to relieve his solitude by practicing upon his biwa. Midnight passed; and the priest did not appear. But the atmosphere was still too warm for comfort within doors; and Hōïchi remained outside. At last he heard steps approaching from the back gate. Somebody crossed the garden, advanced to the veranda, and halted directly in front of him—but it was not the priest. A deep voice called the blind man's name—abruptly and unceremoniously, in the manner of a samurai summoning an inferior:

"Hōïchi!"

Hōïchi was too much startled, for the moment, to respond; and the voice called again, in a tone of harsh command:

"Hōïchi!"

"*Hai!*" answered the blind man, frightened by the menace in the voice—"I am blind!—I cannot know who calls!"

"There is nothing to fear," the stranger exclaimed, speaking more gently. "I am stopping near this temple, and have been sent to you with a message. My present lord, a person of exceedingly high rank is now staying in Akamagaséki, with many noble attendants. He wished to view the scene of the battle of Dan-no-ura; and to-day he visited that place. Having heard of your skill in reciting the story of the battle, he now desires to hear your performance: so you will take your biwa and come with me at once to the house where the august assembly is waiting."

In those times, the order of a samurai was not to be lightly disobeyed. Hōïchi donned his sandals, took his biwa, and went away with the stranger, who guided him deftly, but obliged him to walk very fast. The hand that guided was iron; and the clank of the warrior's stride proved him fully armed—probably some palace-guard on duty. Hōïchi's first alarm was over; he began to imagine himself in good luck; for, remembering the retainer's assurance about a "person of exceedingly high rank", he thought that the lord who wished to hear the recitation could not be less than a daimyō of the first class. Presently the samurai halted; and Hōïchi became aware that they had arrived at a large gateway; and he wondered, for he could not remember any large gate in that part of the town, except the main gate of the Amidaji.

"*Kaimon!*"[1] the samurai called—and there was a sound of unbarring; and the twain passed on. They traversed a space of garden, and halted again before some entrance; and the retainer cried in a loud voice, "Within there! I have brought Hōïchi." Then came sounds of feet hurrying, and screens sliding, and rain-doors opening, and voices of women in converse. By the language of the women Hōïchi knew them to be domestics in some noble household; but he could not imagine to what place he had been conducted. Little time was allowed him for conjecture. After he had been helped to mount several stone steps, upon the last of which he was told to leave his sandals, a woman's hand guided him along interminable reaches of polished planking, and round pillared angles too many to remember, and over widths amazing of matted floor—into the middle of some vast apartment. There he thought that many great people were assembled: the sound of the rustling of silk was like the sound of leaves in a forest. He heard also a great humming of voices—talking in undertones; and the speech was the speech of courts.

Hōïchi was told to put himself at ease, and he found a kneeling-cushion ready for him. After having taken his place upon it, and tuned his instrument, the voice of a woman—whom he divined to be the *Rōjo,* or matron in charge of the female service—addressed him, saying:

"It is now required that the history of the Heiké be recited, to the accompaniment of the biwa."

Now the entire recital would have required a time of many nights; therefore Hōïchi ventured a question:

"As the whole of the story is not soon told, what portion is it augustly desired that I now recite?"

The woman's voice made answer:

"Recite the story of the battle at Dan-no-ura—for the pity of it is the most deep."[2]

[1] A respectful term, signifying the opening of a gate. It was used by samurai when calling to the guards on duty at a lord's gate for admission.

[2] Or the phrase might be rendered, "for the pity of that part is the deepest". The Japanese word for pity in the original text is *awaré.*

Then Hōïchi lifted up his voice, and chanted the chant of the fight on the bitter sea—wonderfully making his biwa to sound like the straining of oars and the rushing of ships, the whirr and the hissing of arrows, the shouting and trampling of men, the crashing of steel upon helmets, the plunging of slain in the flood. And to left and right of him, in the pauses of his playing, he could hear voices murmuring praise: "How marvelous an artist!"—"Never in our own province was playing heard like this!"—"Not in all the empire is there another singer like Hōïchi!" Then fresh courage came to him, and he played and sang yet better than before; and a hush of wonder deepened about him. But when at last he came to tell the fate of the fair and helpless—the piteous perishing of the women and children—and the death-leap of Nii-no-Ama, with the imperial infant in her arms—then all the listeners uttered together one long, long shuddering cry of anguish; and thereafter they wept and wailed so loudly and so wildly that the blind man was frightened by the violence of the grief that he had made. For much time the sobbing and the wailing continued. But gradually the sounds of lamentation died away; and again, in the great stillness that followed, Hōïchi heard the voice of the woman whom he supposed to be the Rōjo.

She said:

"Although we had been assured that you were a very skillful player upon the biwa, and without an equal in recitative, we did not know that anyone could be so skillful as you have proved yourself to-night. Our lord has been pleased to say that he intends to bestow upon you a fitting reward. But he desires that you shall perform before him once every night for the next six nights—after which time he will probably make his august return-journey. To-morrow night, therefore, you are to come here at the same hour. The retainer who to-night conducted you will be sent for you. . . . There is another matter about which I have been ordered to inform you. It is required that you shall speak to no one of your visits here, during the time of our lord's august sojourn at Akamagaséki. As he is traveling incognito,[1] he commands that no mention of these things be made. . . . You are now free to go back to your temple."

After Hōïchi had duly expressed his thanks, a woman's hand conducted him to the entrance of the house, where the same retainer, who had before guided him, was waiting to take him home. The retainer led him to the veranda at the rear of the temple and there bade him farewell.

It was almost dawn when Hōïchi returned; but his absence from the temple had not been observed—as the priest, coming back at a very late hour, had supposed him asleep. During the day Hōïchi was able to take some rest; and he said nothing about his strange adventure. In the middle of the following night the samurai again came for him, and led him to the august assembly, where he gave another recitation with the same success that had attended his previous performance. But during this second visit his absence from the temple was accidentally discovered; and after his return in the morning he was summoned to the presence of the priest, who said to him, in a tone of kindly reproach:

"We have been very anxious about you, friend Hōïchi. To go out, blind and alone, at so late an hour, is dangerous. Why did you go without telling us? I could have ordered a servant to accompany you. And where have you been?"

Hōïchi answered, evasively:

"Pardon me, kind friend! I had to attend to some private business; and I could not arrange the matter at any other hour."

The priest was surprised, rather than pained, by Hōïchi's reticence: he felt it to be unnatural, and suspected something wrong. He feared that the blind lad had been bewitched or deluded by some evil spirits. He did not ask any more questions; but he privately instructed the men-servants of the temple to keep watch upon Hōïchi's movements, and to follow him in case that he should again leave the temple after dark.

[1] "Traveling incognito" is at least the meaning of the original phrase—"making a disguised august-journey" (*shinobi no go-ryokō*).

On the very next night, Hōïchi was seen to leave the temple; and the servants immediately lighted their lanterns, and followed after him. But it was a rainy night, and very dark; and before the temple-folks could get to the roadway, Hōïchi had disappeared. Evidently he had walked very fast—a strange thing, considering his blindness; for the road was in a bad condition. The men hurried through the streets, making inquiries at every house which Hōïchi was accustomed to visit; but nobody could give them any news of him. At last, as they were returning to the temple by way of the shore, they were startled by the sound of a biwa, furiously played, in the cemetery of the Amidaji. Except for some ghostly fires—such as usually flitted there on dark nights—all was blackness in that direction. But the men at once hastened to the cemetery; and, there, by the help of their lanterns, they discovered Hōïchi,—sitting alone in the rain before the memorial tomb of Antoku Tennō, making his biwa resound, and loudly chanting the chant of the battle of Dan-no-ura. And behind him, and about him, and everywhere above the tombs, the fires of the dead were burning, like candles. Never before had so great a host of *Oni-bi* appeared in the sight of mortal man. . . .

"Hōïchi San!—Hōïchi San!" the servants cried—"you are bewitched! . . . Hōïchi San!"

But the blind man did not seem to hear. Strenuously he made his biwa to rattle and ring and clang—more and more wildly he changed the chant of the battle of Dan-no-ura. They caught hold of him—they shouted into his ear:

"Hōïchi San!—Hōïchi San!—come home with us at once!"

Reprovingly he spoke to them:

"To interrupt me in such a manner before this august assembly will not be tolerated."

Whereat, in spite of the weirdness of the thing, the servants could not help laughing. Sure that he had been bewitched, they now seized him, and pulled him up on his feet, and by main force hurried him back to the temple—where he was immediately relieved of his wet clothes, by order of the priest, and reclad, and made to eat and drink. Then the priest insisted upon a full explanation of his friend's astonishing behavior.

Hōïchi long hesitated to speak. But at last, finding that his conduct had really alarmed and angered the good priest, he decided to abandon his reserve; and he related everything that had happened from the time of the first visit of the samurai.

The priest said:

"Hōïchi, my poor friend, you are now in great danger! How unfortunate that you did not tell me all this before! Your wonderful skill in music has indeed brought you into strange trouble. By this time you must be aware that you have not been visiting any house whatever, but have been passing your nights in the cemetery, among the tombs of the Heiké;—and it was before the memorial-tomb of Antoku Tennō that our people to-night found you, sitting in the rain. All that you have been imagining was illusion—except the calling of the dead. By once obeying them, you have put yourself in their power. If you obey them again, after what has already occurred, they will tear you in pieces. But they would have destroyed you, sooner or later, in any event. . . . Now I shall not be able to remain with you to-night: I am called away to perform another service. But, before I go, it will be necessary to protect your body by writing holy texts upon it."

Before sundown the priest and his acolyte stripped Hōïchi: then, with their writing-brushes, they traced upon his breast and back, head and face and neck, limbs and hands and feet—even upon the soles of his feet, and upon all parts of his body—the text of the holy sûtra called *Hannya-Shin-Kyō*.[1] When this had been done, the priest instructed Hōïchi, saying:

"To-night, as soon as I go away, you must seat yourself on the veranda, and wait. You will be called. But, whatever may happen, do not answer, and do not move. Say nothing, and sit

[1]The Smaller Pragña-Pâramitâ-Hridaya-Sûtra is thus called in Japanese. Both the smaller and larger sûtras called Pragña-Pâramitâ ("Transcendent Wisdom") have been translated by the later Professor Max Müller, and can be found in volume xlix. of the *Sacred Books of the East* ("Buddhist Mahâyâna Sûtras").—Apropos of the magical use of the text, as described in this story, it is worth remarking that the subject of the sûtra is the Doctrine of the Emptiness of Forms—that is to say, of the unreal character of all phenomena or noumena.

still—as if meditating. If you stir, or make any noise, you will be torn asunder. Do not get frightened; and do not think of calling for help—because no help could save you. If you do exactly as I tell you, the danger will pass, and you will have nothing more to fear."

After dark the priest and the acolyte went away; and Hōïchi seated himself on the veranda, according to the instructions given him. He laid his biwa on the planking beside him, and assuming the attitude of meditation, remained quite still—taking care not to cough, or to breathe audibly. For hours he stayed thus.

Then, from the roadway, he heard the steps coming. They passed the gate, crossed the garden, approached the veranda, stopped—directly in front of him.

"Hōïchi!" the deep voice called. But the blind man held his breath, and sat motionless.

"Hōïchi!" grimly called the voice a second time. Then a third time—savagely:

"Hōïchi!"

Hōïchi remained as still as a stone and the voice grumbled:

"No answer!—that won't do! . . . Must see where the fellow is."

There was a noise of heavy feet mounting upon the veranda. The feet approached deliberately—halted beside him. Then, for long minutes—during which Hōïchi felt his whole body shake to the beating of his heart—there was dead silence.

At last the gruff voice muttered close to him:

"Here is the biwa; but of the biwa-player I see—only two ears! . . . So that explains why he did not answer: he had no mouth to answer with—there is nothing left of him but his ears.

. . . "Form is emptiness; and emptiness is form. Emptiness is not different from form; form is not different from emptiness. What is form—that is emptiness. What is emptiness—that is form. . . . Perception, name, concept, and knowledge are also emptiness. . . . There is no eye, ear, nose, tongue, body, and mind. . . . But when the envelopment of consciousness has been annihilated, then he [*the seeker*] becomes free from all fear, and beyond the reach of change, enjoying final Nirvâna."

. . . Now to my lord those ears I will take—in proof that the august commands have been obeyed so far as was possible."

At that instant Hōïchi felt his ears gripped by fingers of iron, and torn off! Great as the pain was, he gave no cry. The heavy footfalls receded along the veranda—descended into the garden—passed out to the roadway—ceased. From either side of his head, the blind man felt a thick warm trickling; but he dared not lift his hands. . . .

Before sunrise the priest came back. He hastened at once to the veranda in the rear, stepped and slipped upon something clammy, and uttered a cry of horror—for he saw, by the light of his lantern, that the clamminess was blood. But he perceived Hōïchi sitting there, in the attitude of meditation—with the blood still oozing from his wounds.

"My poor Hōïchi!" cried the startled priest—"what is this? . . . You have been hurt?" . . .

At the sound of his friend's voice, the blind man felt safe. He burst out sobbing, and tearfully told his adventure of the night.

"Poor, poor Hōïchi!" the priest exclaimed—"all my fault!—my very grievous fault! . . . Everywhere upon your body the holy texts had been written—except upon your ears! I trusted my acolyte to do that part of the work; and it was very, very wrong of me not to have made sure that he had done it! . . . Well, the matter cannot now be helped—we can only try to heal your hurts as soon as possible. Cheer up, friend!—the danger is now well over. You will never again be troubled by those visitors."

With the aid of a good doctor, Hōïchi soon recovered from his injuries. The story of his strange adventure spread far and wide, and soon made him famous. Many noble persons went to Akamagaséki to hear him recite; and large presents of money were given to him—so that he became a wealthy man. . . . But from the time of his adventure, he was known only by the appellation of *Mimi-nashi-Hōïchi:* "Hōïchi-the-Earless."

OSHIDORI

Oshidori

Oshidori

There was a falconer and hunter, named Sonjō, who lived in the district called Tamura-no-Gō, of the province of Mutsu. One day he went out hunting, and could not find any game. But on his way home, at a place called Akanuma, he perceived a pair of *oshidori*[1] (mandarin-ducks) swimming together in a river that he was about to cross. To kill *oshidori* is not good; but Sonjō happened to be very hungry, and he shot at the pair. His arrow pierced the male: the female escaped into the rushes of the further shore, and disappeared. Sonjō took the dead bird home and cooked it.

That night he dreamed a dreary dream. It seemed to him that a beautiful woman came into his room, and stood by his pillow, and began to weep. So bitterly did she weep that Sonjō felt as if his heart were being torn out while he listened. And the woman cried to him: "Why—oh! why did you kill him?—of what wrong was he guilty? . . . At Akanuma we were so happy together—and you killed him! . . . What harm did he ever do you? Do you even know what you have done?—oh! do you know what a cruel, what a wicked thing you have done? . . . Me too you have killed—for I will not live without my husband! . . . Only to tell you this I came." . . . Then again she wept aloud—so bitterly that the voice of her crying pierced into the marrow of the listener's bones—and she sobbed out the words of this poem:

[1] From ancient time, in the Far East, these birds have been regarded as emblems of conjugal affection.

Hi kururéba
Sasoëshi mono wo—
Akanuma no
Makomo no kuré no
Hitori-né zo uki!

[*"At the coming of twilight I invited him to return with me—! Now to sleep alone in the shadow of the rushes of Akanuma—ah! what misery unspeakable!"*][1]

And after having uttered these verses she exclaimed:—"Ah, you do not know—you cannot know what you have done! But to-morrow, when you go to Akanuma, you will see—you will see. . . ." So saying, and weeping very piteously, she went away.

When Sonjō awoke in the morning, this dream remained so vivid in his mind that he was greatly troubled. He remembered the words:—"But to-morrow, when you go to Akanuma, you will see—you will see." And he resolved to go there at once, that he might learn whether his dream was anything more than a dream.

So he went to Akanuma; and there, when he came to the river-bank, he saw the female *oshidori* swimming alone. In the same moment the bird perceived Sonjō; but, instead of trying to escape, she swam straight toward him, looking at him the while in a strange fixed way. Then, with her beak, she suddenly tore open her own body, and died before the hunter's eyes. . . .

Sonjō shaved his head, and became a priest.

[1]There is a pathetic double meaning in the third verse; for the syllables composing the proper name *Akanuma* ("Red Marsh") may also be read as *akanu-ma*, signifying "the time of our inseparable (or delightful) relation". So the poem can also be thus rendered:—"When the day began to fail, I had invited him to accompany me. . . . ! Now, after the time of that happy relation, what misery for the one who must slumber alone in the shadow of the rushes!"—The *makomo* is a sort of a large rush, used for making baskets.

THE STORY OF O-TEI

The Story of O-Tei

The Story of O-Tei

A long time ago, in the town of Niigata, in the province of Echizen, there lived a man called Nagao Chōsei.

Nagao was the son of a physician, and was educated for his father's profession. At an early age he had been betrothed to a girl called O-Tei, the daughter of one of his father's friends; and both families had agreed that the wedding should take place as soon as Nagao had finished his studies. But the health of O-Tei proved to be weak; and in her fifteenth year she was attacked by a fatal consumption. When she became aware that she must die, she sent for Nagao to bid him farewell.

As he knelt at her bedside, she said to him:

"Nagao-Sama, my betrothed, we were promised to each other from the time of our childhood; and we were to have been married at the end of this year. But now I am going to die—the gods know what is best for us. If I were able to live for some years longer, I could only continue to be a cause of trouble and grief to others. With this frail body, I could not be a good wife; and therefore even to wish to live, for your sake, would be a very selfish wish. I am quite resigned to die; and I want you to promise that you will not grieve. . . . Besides, I want to tell you that I think we shall meet again." . . .

"Indeed we shall meet again," Nagao answered earnestly. "And in that Pure Land there will be no pain of separation."

"Nay, nay!" she responded softly, "I meant not the Pure

Land. I believe that we are destined to meet again in this world—although I shall be buried to-morrow."

Nagao looked at her wonderingly, and saw her smile at his wonder. She continued, in her gentle, dreamy voice:

"Yes, I mean in this world—in your own present life, Nagao-Sama. . . . Providing, indeed, that you wish it. Only, for this thing to happen, I must again be born a girl, and grow up to womanhood. So you would have to wait. Fifteen—sixteen years: that is a long time. . . . But, my promised husband, you are now only nineteen years old." . . .

Eager to soothe her dying moments, he answered tenderly:

"To wait for you, my betrothed, were no less a joy than a duty. We are pledged to each other for the time of seven existences."

"But you doubt?" she questioned, watching his face.

"My dear one," he answered, "I doubt whether I should be able to know you in another body, under another name—unless you can tell me of a sign or token."

"That I cannot do," she said. "Only the Gods and the Buddhas know how and where we shall meet. But I am sure—very, very sure—that, if you be not unwilling to receive me, I shall be able to come back to you. . . . Remember these words of mine." . . .

She ceased to speak; and her eyes closed. She was dead.

*

* *

Nagao had been sincerely attached to O-Tei; and his grief was deep. He had a mortuary tablet made, inscribed with her *zokumyō*;[1] and he placed the tablet in his *butsudan*,[2] and every day set offerings before it. He thought a great deal about the strange things that O-Tei had said to him just before her death;

[1]The Buddhist term *zokumyō* ("profane name") signifies the personal name, borne during life, in contradistinction to the *kaimyō* ("sila-name") or *homyō* ("Law-name") given after death—religious posthumous appellations inscribed upon the tomb, and upon the mortuary tablet in the parish-temple.—For some account of these, see my paper entitled, "The Literature of the Dead," in *Exotics and Retrospectives*.

[2]Buddhist household shrine.

and, in the hope of pleasing her spirit, he wrote a solemn promise to wed her if she could ever return to him in another body. This written promise he sealed with his seal, and placed in the *butsudan* beside the mortuary tablet of O-Tei.

Nevertheless, as Nagao was an only son, it was necessary that he should marry. He soon found himself obliged to yield to the wishes of his family, and to accept a wife of his father's choosing. After his marriage he continued to set offerings before the tablet of O-Tei; and he never failed to remember her with affection. But by degrees her image became dim in his memory—like a dream that is hard to recall. And the years went by.

During those years many misfortunes came upon him. He lost his parents by death,—then his wife and his only child. So that he found himself alone in the world. He abandoned his desolate home, and set out upon a long journey in the hope of forgetting his sorrows.

One day, in the course of his travels, he arrived at Ikao—a mountain-village still famed for its thermal springs, and for the beautiful scenery of its neighborhood. In the village-inn at which he stopped, a young girl came to wait upon him; and, at the first sight of her face, he felt his heart leap as it had never leaped before. So strangely did she resemble O-Tei that he pinched himself to make sure that he was not dreaming. As she went and came—bringing fire and food, or arranging the chamber of the guest—her every attitude and motion revived in him some gracious memory of the girl to whom he had been pledged in his youth. He spoke to her; and she responded in a soft, clear voice of which the sweetness saddened him with a sadness of other days.

Then, in great wonder, he questioned her, saying:

"Elder Sister, so much do you look like a person whom I knew long ago, that I was startled when you first entered this room. Pardon me, therefore, for asking what is your native place, and what is your name?"

Immediately—and in the unforgotten voice of the dead—she thus made answer:

"My name is O-Tei; and you are Nagao Chōsei of Echigo, my promised husband. Seventeen years ago, I died in Niigata: then you made in writing a promise to marry me if ever I could come back to this world in the body of a woman—and you sealed that written promise with your seal, and put it in the *butsudan*, beside the tablet inscribed with my name. And therefore I came back." . . .

As she uttered these last words, she fell unconscious.

Nagao married her; and the marriage was a happy one. But at no time afterward could she remember what she had told him in answer to his question at Ikao: neither could she remember anything of her previous existence. The recollection of the former birth—mysteriously kindled in the moment of that meeting—had again become obscured, and so thereafter remained.

UBAZAKURA

Ubazakura

Ubazakura

Three hundred years ago, in the village called Asamimura, in the district called Onsengōri, in the province of Iyō, there lived a good man named Tokubei. This Tokubei was the richest person in the district, and the *muraosa,* or headman, of the village. In most matters he was fortunate; but he reached the age of forty without knowing the happiness of becoming a father. Therefore he and his wife, in the affliction of their childlessness, addressed many prayers to the divinity Fudō Myō Ō, who had a famous temple, called Saihōji, in Asamimura.

At last their prayers were heard: the wife of Tokubei gave birth to a daughter. The child was very pretty; and she received the name of Tsuyu. As the mother's milk was deficient, a milk-nurse, called O-Sodé, was hired for the little one.

O-Tsuyu grew up to be a very beautiful girl; but at the age of fifteen she fell sick, and the doctors thought that she was going to die. In that time the nurse O-Sodé, who loved O-Tsuyu with a real mother's love, went to the temple Saihōji, and fervently prayed to Fudō-Sama on behalf of the girl. Every day, for twenty-one days, she went to the temple and prayed; and at the end of that time, O-Tsuyu suddenly and completely recovered.

Then there was great rejoicing in the house of Tokubei; and he gave a feast to all his friends in celebration of the happy event. But on the night of the feast the nurse O-Sodé was suddenly taken ill; and on the following morning, the doctor, who had been summoned to attend her, announced that she was dying.

Then the family, in great sorrow, gathered about her bed, to bid her farewell. But she said to them:

"It is time that I should tell you something which you do not know. My prayer has been heard. I besought Fudō-Sama that I might be permitted to die in the place of O-Tsuyu; and this great favor has been granted me. Therefore you must not grieve about my death. . . . But I have one request to make. I promised Fudō-Sama that I would have a cherry-tree planted in the garden of Saihōji, for a thank-offering and a commemoration. Now I shall not be able myself to plant the tree there: so I must beg that you will fulfill that vow for me. . . . Good-bye, dear friends; and remember that I was happy to die for O-Tsuyu's sake."

After the funeral of O-Sodé, a young cherry tree—the finest that could be found—was planted in the garden of Saihōji by the parents of O-Tsuyu. The tree grew and flourished; and on the sixteenth day of the second month of the following year—the anniversary of O-Sodé's death—it blossomed in a wonderful way. So it continued to blossom for two hundred and fifty-four years—always upon the sixteenth day of the second month—and its flowers, pink and white, were like the nipples of a woman's breast, bedewed with milk. And the people called it *Ubazakura,* the Cherry-tree of the Milk-Nurse.

Diplomacy

Diplomacy

Diplomacy

It had been ordered that the execution should take place in the garden of the *yashiki.* So the man was taken there, and made to kneel down in a wide sanded space crossed by a line of *tobi-ishi,* or stepping-stones, such as you may still see in Japanese landscape-gardens. His arms were bound behind him. Retainers brought water in buckets, and rice-bags filled with pebbles; and they packed the rice-bags round the kneeling man—so wedging him in that he could not move. The master came, and observed the arrangements. He found them satisfactory, and made no remarks.

Suddenly the condemned may cried out to him:

"Honored Sir, the fault for which I have been doomed I did not wittingly commit. It was only my very great stupidity which caused the fault. Having been born stupid, by reason of my Karma, I could not always help making mistakes. But to kill a man for being stupid is wrong—and that wrong will be repaid. So surely as you kill me, so surely shall I be avenged—out of the resentment that you provoke will come the vengeance; and evil will be rendered for evil." . . .

If any person be killed while feeling strong resentment, the ghost of that person will be able to take vengeance upon the killer. This the samurai knew. He replied very gently,—almost caressingly:

"We shall allow you to frighten us as much as you please—after you are dead. But it is difficult to believe that you mean what you say. Will you try to give some sign of your great resentment—after your head has been cut off?"

"Assuredly I will," answered the man.

"Very well," said the samurai, drawing his long sword. "I am now going to cut off your head. Directly in front of you there is a stepping-stone. After your head has been cut off, try to bite the stepping-stone. If your angry ghost can help you to do that, some of us may be frightened. . . . Will you try to bite the stone?"

"I will bite it!" cried the man, in great anger—"I will bite it!—I will bite"—

There was a flash, a swish, a crunching thud: the bound body bowed over the rice sacks—two long blood-jets pumping from the shorn neck—and the head rolled upon the sand. Heavily toward the stepping-stone it rolled: then, suddenly bounding, it caught the upper edge of the stone between its teeth, clung desperately for a moment, and dropped inert.

None spoke; but the retainers stared in horror at their master. He seemed to be quite unconcerned. He merely held out his sword to the nearest attendant, who, with a wooden dipper, poured water over the blade from haft to point, and then carefully wiped the steel several times with sheets of soft paper. . . . And thus ended the ceremonial part of the incident.

For months thereafter, the retainers and the domestics lived in ceaseless fear of ghostly visitation. None of them doubted that the promised vengeance would come; and their constant terror caused them to hear and to see much that did not exist. They became afraid of the sound of the wind in the bamboos—afraid even of the stirring of shadows in the garden. At last, after taking counsel together, they decided to petition their master to have a *Ségaki*-service performed on behalf of the vengeful spirit.

"Quite unnecessary," the samurai said, when his chief retainer had uttered the general wish. . . . "I understand that the desire of a dying man for revenge may be a cause for fear. But in this case there is nothing to fear."

The retainer looked at his master beseechingly, but hesitated to ask the reason of this alarming confidence.

"Oh, the reason is simple enough," declared the samurai, divining the unspoken doubt. "Only the very last intention of that fellow could have been dangerous; and when I challenged him to give me the sign, I diverted his mind from the desire of revenge. He died with the set purpose of biting the stepping-stone; and that purpose he was able to accomplish, but nothing else. All the rest he must have forgotten. . . . So you need not feel any further anxiety about the matter."

—And indeed the dead man gave no more trouble. Nothing at all happened.

OF A MIRROR AND A BELL

Of a Mirror and a Bell

Of a Mirror and a Bell

Eight centuries ago, the priests of Mugenyama, in the province of Tōtōmi, wanted a big bell for their temple; and they asked the women of their parish to help them by contributing old bronze mirrors for bell-metal.

[Even to-day, in the courts of certain Japanese temples, you may see heaps of old bronze mirrors contributed for such a purpose. The largest collection of this kind that I ever saw was in the court of a temple of the Jōdo sect, at Hakata, in Kyūshū: the mirrors had been given for the making of a bronze statue of Amida, thirty-three feet high.]

There was at that time a young woman, a farmer's wife, living at Mugenyama, who presented her mirror to the temple, to be used for bell-metal. But afterward she much regretted her mirror. She remembered things that her mother had told her about it; and she remembered that it had belonged, not only to her mother but to her mother's mother and grandmother; and she remembered some happy smiles which it had reflected. Of course, if she could have offered the priests a certain sum of money in place of the mirror, she could have asked them to give back her heirloom. But she had not the money necessary. Whenever she went to the temple, she saw her mirror lying in the court-yard, behind a railing, among hundreds of other mirrors heaped there together. She knew it by the *Shō-Chiku-Bai* in relief on the back of it—those three fortunate emblems of Pine, Bamboo, and Plumflower, which delighted her baby-eyes when her mother first showed her the mirror. She longed for some chance to steal the mirror, and hide it—that she might thereafter treasure it always. But the chance did not come; and she became very unhappy—felt as if she had foolishly given away a part of her life. She thought about the old saying that a mirror is the Soul of a Woman—(a saying mystically expressed, by the Chinese character for Soul, upon the backs of many bronze mirrors)—and she feared that it was true in weirder ways than she had before imagined. But she could not dare to speak of her pain to anybody.

Now, when all the mirrors contributed for the Mugenyama bell had been sent to the foundry, the bell-founders discovered that there was one mirror among them which would not melt. Again and again they tried to melt it; but it resisted all their efforts. Evidently the woman who had given that mirror to the temple must have regretted the giving. She had not presented her offering with all her heart; and therefore her selfish soul, remaining attached to the mirror, kept it hard and cold in the midst of the furnace.

Of course everybody heard of the matter, and everybody soon knew whose mirror it was that would not melt. And because of this public exposure of her secret fault, the poor woman became very much ashamed and very angry. And as she could not bear the shame, she drowned herself, after having written a farewell letter containing these words:

"When I am dead, it will not be difficult to melt the mirror and to cast the bell. But, to the person who breaks that bell by ringing it, great wealth will be given by the ghost of me."

—You must know that the last wish or promise of anybody who dies in anger, or performs suicide in anger, is generally supposed to possess a supernatural force. After the dead woman's mirror had been melted, and the bell had been successfully cast, people remembered the words of that letter. They felt sure that the spirit of the writer would give wealth to the breaker of the bell; and, as soon as the bell had been suspended in the court of the temple, they went in multitude to ring it. With all their might and main they swung the ringing beam; but the bell proved to be a good bell, and it bravely withstood their assaults. Nevertheless, the people were not easily discouraged. Day after day, at all hours, they continued to ring the bell furiously—caring nothing whatever for the protests of the priests. So the ringing became an affliction; and the priests could not endure it; and they got rid of the bell by rolling it down the hill into a swamp. The swamp was deep, and swallowed it up—and that was the end of the bell. Only its legend remains; and in that legend it is called the *Mugen-Kané,* or Bell of Mugen.

*

* *

Now there are queer old Japanese beliefs in the magical efficacy of a certain mental operation implied, though not described, by the verb *nazoraëru.* The word itself cannot be adequately rendered by any English word; for it is used in relation to many kinds of mimetic magic, as well as in relation to the performance of many religious acts of faith. Common meanings of *nazoraëru,* according to dictionaries, are "to imitate", "to compare", "to liken"; but the esoteric meaning is *to substitute, in imagination, one object or action for another, so as to bring about some magical or miraculous result.*

For example: you cannot afford to build a Buddhist temple; but you can easily lay a pebble before the image of the Buddha, with the same pious feeling that would prompt you to build a temple if you were rich enough to build one. The merit of so offering the pebble becomes equal, or almost equal, to the merit of erecting a temple. . . . You cannot read the six thousand seven hundred and seventy-one volumes of the Buddhist texts; but you can make a revolving library, containing them, turn round, by pushing it like a windlass. And if you push with an earnest wish that you could read the six thousand seven hundred and seventy-one volumes, you will acquire the same merit as the reading of them would enable you to gain. . . .

So much will perhaps suffice to explain the religious meanings of *nazoraëru.*

The magical meanings could not all be explained without a great variety of examples; but, for present purposes, the following will serve. If you should make a little man of straw, for the same reason that Sister Helen made a little man of wax—and nail it, with nails not less than five inches long, to some tree in a temple-grove at the Hour of the Ox—and if the person, imaginatively represented by that little straw man, should die thereafter in fearful agony—that would illustrate one signification of *nazoraëru.* . . . Or, let us suppose that a robber has entered your house during the night and carried away your valuables. If you can discover the footprints of that robber in your garden, and then promptly burn a very large moxa on each of them, the soles of the feet of the robber will become inflamed, and will allow him no rest until he returns, of his own accord, to put himself at your mercy. That is another kind of mimetic magic expressed by the term *nazoraëru.* And a third kind is illustrated by various legends of the Mugen-Kané.

*

* *

After the bell had been rolled into the swamp, there was, of course, no more chance of ringing it in such wise as to break it. But persons who regretted this loss of opportunity would strike and break objects imaginatively substituted for the bell—thus hoping to please the spirit of the owner of the mirror that had made so much trouble. One of these persons was a woman called Umégaë—famed in Japanese legend because of her relation to Kajiwara Kagésué, a warrior of the Heiké clan. While the pair were traveling together, Kajiwara one day found himself in great straits for want of money; and Umégaë, remembering the tradition of the Bell of Mugen, took a basin of bronze, and, mentally representing it to be the bell, beat upon it until she broke it—crying out, at the same time, for three hundred pieces of gold. A guest of the inn where the pair were stopping made inquiry as to the cause of the banging and the crying, and, on learning the story of the trouble, actually presented Umégaë with three hundred *ryō* in gold. Afterward a song was made about Umégaë's basin of bronze; and that song is sung by dancing girls even to this day:

> Umégaë no chōzubachi tataïté
> O-kané ga déru naraba,
> Mina San mi-uké wo
> Sōré tanomimasu.

[*"If, by striking upon the wash-basin of Umégaë, I could make honorable money come to me, then would I negotiate for the freedom of all my girl-comrades."*]

After this happening, the fame of the Mugen-Kané became great; and many people followed the example of Umégaë—thereby hoping to emulate her luck. Among these folk was a dissolute farmer who lived near Mugenyama, on the bank of the Ōïgawa. Having wasted his substance in riotous living, this farmer made for himself, out of the mud in his garden, a clay-model of the Mugen-Kané; and he beat the clay-bell, and broke it—crying out the while for great wealth.

Then, out of the ground before him, rose up the figure of a white-robed woman, with long, loose-flowing hair, holding a covered jar. And the woman said: "I have come to answer your fervent prayer as it deserves to be answered. Take, therefore, this jar." So saying, she put the jar into his hands, and disappeared.

Into his house the happy man rushed, to tell his wife the good news. He set down in front of her the covered jar—which was heavy—and they opened it together. And they found that it was filled, up to the very brim, with . . .

But, no!—I really cannot tell you with what it was filled.

JIKININKI

Jikininki

Jikininki

Once, when Musō Kokushi, a priest of the Zen sect, was journeying alone through the province of Mino, he lost his way in a mountain-district where there was nobody to direct him. For a long time he wandered about helplessly; and he was beginning to despair of finding shelter for the night, when he perceived, on the top of a hill lighted by the last rays of the sun, one of those little hermitages, called *anjitsu,* which are built for solitary priests. It seemed to be in a ruinous condition; but he hastened to it eagerly, and found that it was inhabited by an aged priest, from whom he begged the favor of a night's lodging. This the old man harshly refused; but he directed Musō to a certain hamlet, in a valley adjoining, where lodging and food could be obtained.

Musō found his way to the hamlet, which consisted of less than a dozen farm-cottages; and he was kindly received at the dwelling of the headman. Forty or fifty persons were assembled in the principal apartment, at the moment of Musō's arrival; but he was shown into a small separate room, where he was promptly supplied with food and bedding. Being very tired, he lay down to rest at an early hour; but a little before midnight he was roused from sleep by a sound of loud weeping in the next apartment. Presently the sliding-screens were gently pushed apart; and a young man, carrying a lighted lantern, entered the room, respectfully saluted him, and said:

"Reverend Sir, it is my painful duty to tell you that I am

now the responsible head of this house. Yesterday I was only the eldest son. But when you came here, tired as you were, we did not wish that you should feel embarrassed in any way: therefore we did not tell you that father had died only a few hours before. The people whom you saw in the next room are the inhabitants of this village: they are all assembled here to pay their last respects to the dead; and now they are going to another village, about three miles off—for, by our custom, no one of us may remain in this village during the night after a death has taken place. We make the proper offerings and prayers; then we go away, leaving the corpse alone. Strange things always happen in the house where a corpse has thus been left: so we think that it will be better for you to come away with us. We can find you good lodging in the other village. But perhaps, as you are a priest, you have no fear of demons or evil spirits; and, if you are not afraid of being left alone with the body, you will be very welcome to the use of this poor house. However, I must tell you that nobody, except a priest, would dare to remain here tonight."

Musō made answer:

"For your kind intention and your generous hospitality, I am deeply grateful. But I am sorry that you did not tell me of your father's death when I came; for, though I was a little tired, I certainly was not so tired that I should have found any difficulty in doing my duty as a priest. Had you told me, I could have performed the service before your departure. As it is, I shall perform the service after you have gone away; and I shall stay by the body until morning. I do not know what you mean by your words about the danger of staying here alone; but I am not afraid of ghosts or demons: therefore please do not have any anxiety on my account."

The young man appeared to be rejoiced by these assurances, and expressed his gratitude in fitting words. Then the other members of the family, and the folk assembled in the adjoining room, having been told of the priest's kind promises, came to thank him—after which the master of the house said:

"Now, reverend Sir, much as we regret to leave you alone,

we must bid you farewell. By the rule of our village, none of us can stay here after midnight. We beg, kind Sir, that you will take every care of your honorable body, while we are unable to attend upon you. And if you happen to hear or see anything strange during our absence, please tell us of the matter when we return in the morning."

All then left the house, except the priest, who went to the room were the dead body was lying. The usual offerings had been set before the corpse; and a small Buddhist lamp—*tōmyō*—was burning. The priest recited the service, and performed the funeral ceremonies—after which he entered into meditation. So meditating he remained through several silent hours; and there was no sound in the deserted village. But, when the hush of the night was at its deepest, there noiselessly entered a Shape, vague and vast; and in the same moment Musō found himself without power to move or speak. He saw that Shape lift the corpse, as with hands, and devour it, more quickly than a cat devours a rat—beginning at the head, and eating everything: the hair and the bones and even the shroud. And the monstrous Thing, having thus consumed the body, turned to the offerings, and ate them also. Then it went away, as mysteriously as it had come.

When the villagers returned next morning, they found the priest awaiting them at the door of the headman's dwelling. All in turn saluted him; and when they had entered, and looked about the room, no one expressed any surprise at the disappearance of the dead body and the offerings. But the master of the house said to Musō:

"Reverend Sir, you have probably seen unpleasant things during the night: all of us were anxious about you. But now we are very happy to find you alive and unharmed. Gladly we would have stayed with you, if it had been possible. But the law of our village, as I told you last evening, obliges us to quit our houses after a death has taken place, and to leave the corpse alone. Whenever this law has been broken, heretofore, some great misfortune has followed. Whenever it is obeyed, we find that the corpse and the offerings disappear during our absence. Perhaps you have seen the cause."

Then Musō told of the dim and awful Shape that had entered the death-chamber to devour the body and the offerings. No person seemed to be surprised by his narration; and the master of the house observed:

"What you have told us, reverend Sir, agrees with what has been said about this matter from ancient time."

Musō then inquired:

"Does not the priest on the hill sometimes perform the funeral-service for your dead?"

"What priest?" the young man asked.

"The priest who yesterday evening directed me to this village," answered Musō. "I called at his *anjitsu* on the hill yonder. He refused me lodging, but told me the way here."

The listeners looked at each other, as in astonishment; and, after a moment of silence, the master of the house said:

"Reverend Sir, there is no priest and there is no *anjitsu* on the hill. For the time of many generations there has not been any resident-priest in this neighborhood."

Musō said nothing more on the subject; for it was evident that his kind hosts supposed him to have been deluded by some goblin. But after having bidden them farewell, and obtained all necessary information as to his road, he determined to look again for the hermitage on the hill, and so to ascertain whether he had really been deceived. He found the *anjitsu* without any difficulty; and, this time, its aged occupant invited him to enter. When he had done so, the hermit humbly bowed down before him, exclaiming:—"Ah! I am ashamed!—I am very much ashamed!—I am exceedingly ashamed!"

"You need not be ashamed for having refused me shelter," said Musō. "You directed me to the village yonder, where I was very kindly treated; and I thank you for that favor."

"I can give no man shelter," the recluse made answer; "and it is not for the refusal that I am ashamed. I am ashamed only that you should have seen me in my real shape,—for it was I who devoured the corpse and the offerings last night before your eyes. ... Know, reverend Sir, that I am a *jikininki*,[1]—an eater of human flesh. Have pity upon me, and suffer me to confess the secret fault by which I became reduced to this condition.

"A long, long time ago, I was a priest in this desolate region. There was no other priest for many leagues around. So, in that time, the bodies of the mountain-folk who died used to be brought here—sometimes from great distances—in order that I might repeat over them the holy service. But I repeated the service and performed the rites only as a matter of business—I thought only of the food and the clothes that my sacred profession enabled me to gain. And because of this selfish impiety I was reborn, immediately after my death, into the state of a *jikininki*. Since then I have been obliged to feed upon the corpses of the people who die in this district: every one of them I must devour in the way that you saw last night. ... Now, reverend Sir, let me beseech you to perform a Ségaki-service[2] for me: help me by your prayers, I entreat you, so that I may be soon able to escape from this horrible state of existence." ...

No sooner had the hermit uttered this petition than he disappeared; and the hermitage also disappeared at the same instant. And Musō Kokushi found himself kneeling alone in the high grass, beside an ancient and moss-grown tomb, of the form called *go-rin-ishi*,[3] which seemed to be the tomb of a priest.

[1]Literally, a man-eating goblin. The Japanese narrator gives also the Sanscrit term, "Râkshasa"; but this word is quite as vague as *jikininki*, since there are many kinds of Râkshasas. Apparently the word *jikininki* signifies here one of the *Baramon-Rasetsu-Gaki*—forming the twenty-sixth class of pretas enumerated in the old Buddhist books.

[2]A *Ségaki*-service is a special Buddhist service performed on behalf of beings supposed to have entered into the condition of *gaki* (pretas), or hungry spirits. For a brief account of such a service, see my *Japanese Miscellany*.

[3]Literally, "five-circle [or 'five-zone'] stone". A funeral monument consisting of five parts superimposed—each of a different form—symbolizing the five mystic elements: Ether, Air, Fire, Water, Earth.

MUJINA

Mujina

Mujina

On the Akasaka Road, in Tōkyō, there is a slope called Kii-no-kuni-zaka—which means the Slope of the Province of Kii. I do not know why it is called the Slope of the Province of Kii. On one side of this slope you see an ancient moat, deep and very wide, with high green banks rising up to some palace gardens;—and on the other side of the road extend the long and lofty walls of an imperial palace. Before the era of street-lamps and jinrikishas, this neighborhood was very lonesome after dark; and belated pedestrians would go miles out of their way rather than mount the Kii-no-kuni-zaka, alone, after sunset.

All because of a Mujina that used to walk there.

The last man who saw the Mujina was an old merchant of the Kyōbashi quarter, who died about thirty years ago. This is the story, as he told it:

One night, at a late hour, he was hurrying up the Kii-no-kuni-zaka, when he perceived a woman crouching by the moat, all alone, and weeping bitterly. Fearing that she intended to drown herself, he stopped to offer her any assistance or consolation in his power. She appeared to be a slight and graceful person, handsomely dressed; and her hair was arranged like that of a young girl of good family. "O-jochū,"[1] he exclaimed, approach-

[1]O-jochū ("honorable damsel") is a polite form of address used in speaking to a young lady whom one does not know.

ing her—"O-jochū, do not cry like that! . . . Tell me what the trouble is; and if there be any way to help you, I shall be glad to help you." (He really meant what he said, for he was a very kind man.) But she continued to weep—hiding her face from him with one of her long sleeves. "O-jochū," he said again, as gently as he could,—"please, please listen to me! . . . This is no place for a young lady at night! Do not cry, I implore you!—only tell me how I may be of some help to you!" Slowly she rose up, but turned her back to him, and continued to moan and sob behind her sleeve. He laid his hand lightly upon her shoulder, and pleaded:—"O-jochū!—O-jochū!—O-jochū! . . . Listen to me, just for one little moment! . . . O-jochū!—O-jochū!" . . . Then that O-jochū turned round, and dropped her sleeve, and stroked her face with her hand;—and the man saw that she had no eyes or nose or mouth,—and he screamed and ran away.

Up Kii-no-kuni-zaka he ran and ran; and all was black and empty before him. On and on he ran, never daring to look back; and at last he saw a lantern, so far away that it looked like the gleam of a firefly; and he made for it. It proved to be only the lantern of an itinerant *soba*-seller,[1] who had set down his stand by the roadside; but any light and any human companionship were good after that experience; and he flung himself down at the feet of the *soba*-seller, crying out, "Aa!—aa!!—*aa!!!*" . . .

"*Koré! koré!*" roughly exclaimed the soba-man. "Here! what is the matter with you? Anybody hurt you?"

"No—nobody hurt me," panted the other—"only . . . *Aa!—aa!*" . . .

"—Only scared you?" queried the peddler, unsympathetically. "Robbers?"

"Not robbers—not robbers," gasped the terrified man. . . . "I saw . . . I saw a woman—by the moat—and she showed me . . . *Aa!* I cannot tell you what she showed me!" . . .

"*Hé!* Was it anything like *this* that she showed you?" cried the soba-man, stroking his own face—which therewith became like unto an Egg. . . . And, simultaneously, the light went out.

[1] *Soba* is a preparation of buckwheat, somewhat resembling vermicelli.

ROKURO-KUBI

Rokuro-Kubi

Rokuro-Kubi

Nearly five hundred years ago there was a samurai, named Isogai Héïdazaëmon Takétsura, in the service of the Lord Kikuji, of Myūshū. This Isogai had inherited, from many warlike ancestors, a natural aptitude for military exercises, and extraordinary strength. While yet a boy he had surpassed his teachers in the art of swordsmanship, in archery, and in the use of the spear, and had displayed all the capacities of a daring and skillful soldier. Afterwards, in the time of the Eikyō[1] war, he so distinguished himself that high honors were bestowed upon him. But when the house of Kikuji came to ruin, Isogai found himself without a master. He might then easily have obtained service under another daimyō; but as he had never sought distinction for his own sake alone, and as his heart remained true to his former lord, he preferred to give up the world. So he cut off his hair, and became a traveling priest—taking the Buddhist name of Kwairyō.

But always, under the *koromo*[2] of the priest, Kwairyō kept warm within him the heart of the samurai. As in other years he had laughed at peril, so now also he scorned danger; and in all weathers and all seasons he journeyed to preach the good Law in places where no other priest would have dared to go. For that age was an age of violence and disorder; and upon the highways

[1]The period of Eikyō lasted from 1429 to 1441.
[2]The upper robe of a Buddhist priest.

there was no security for the solitary traveler, even if he happened to be a priest.

In the course of his first long journey, Kwairyō had occasion to visit the province of Kai. One evening, as he was traveling through the mountains of that province, darkness overtook him in a very lonesome district, leagues away from any village. So he resigned himself to pass the night under the stars; and having found a suitable grassy spot, by the roadside, he lay down there, and prepared to sleep. He had always welcomed discomfort; and even a bare rock was for him a good bed, when nothing better could be found, and the root of a pine-tree an excellent pillow. His body was like iron; and he never troubled himself about dews or rain or frost or snow.

Scarcely had he lain down when a man came along the road, carrying an axe and a great bundle of chopped wood. The woodcutter halted on seeing Kwairyō lying down, and, after a moment of silent observation, said to him in a tone of great surprise:

"What kind of a man can you be, good Sir, that you dare to lie down alone in such a place as this? . . . There are haunters about here—many of them. Are you not afraid of Hairy Things?"

"My friend," cheerfully answered Kwairyō, "I am only a wandering priest—a 'Cloud-and-Water-Guest', as folks call it: *Un-sui-no-ryokaku.* And I am not in the least afraid of Hairy Things—if you mean goblin-foxes, or goblin-badgers, or any creatures of that kind. As for lonesome places, I like them: they are suitable for meditation. I am accustomed to sleeping in the open air: and I have learned never to be anxious about my life."

"You must be indeed a brave man, Sir Priest," the peasant responded, "to lie down here! This place has a bad name—a very bad name. But, as the proverb has it, *Kunshi aya-uki ni chikayorazu* ['The superior man does not needlessly expose himself to peril']; and I must assure you, Sir, that it is very dangerous to sleep here. Therefore, although my house is only a wretched thatched hut, let me beg of you to come home with me at once.

In the way of food, I have nothing to offer you; but there is a roof at least, and you can sleep under it without risk."

He spoke earnestly; and Kwairyō, liking the kindly tone of the man, accepted this modest offer. The woodcutter guided him along a narrow path, leading up from the main road through mountain-forest. It was a rough and dangerous path—sometimes skirting precipices—sometimes offering nothing but a network of slippery roots for the foot to rest upon,—sometimes winding over or between masses of jagged rock. But at last Kwairyō found himself upon a cleared space at the top of a hill, with a full moon shining overhead; and he saw before him a small thatched cottage, cheerfully lighted from within. The woodcutter led him to a shed at the back of the house, whither water had been conducted, through bamboo-pipes, from some neighboring stream; and the two men washed their feet. Beyond the shed was a vegetable garden, and a grove of cedars and bamboos; and beyond the trees appeared the glimmer of a cascade, pouring from some loftier height, and swaying in the moonshine like a long white robe.

As Kwairyō entered the cottage with his guide, he perceived four persons—men and women—warming their hands at a little fire kindled in the *ro*[1] of the principal apartment. They bowed low to the priest, and greeted him in the most respectful manner. Kwairyō wondered that persons so poor, and dwelling in such a solitude, should be aware of the polite forms of greeting. "These are good people," he thought to himself; "and they must have been taught by someone well acquainted with the rules of propriety." Then turning to his host—the *aruji,* or house-master, as the others called him—Kwairyō said:

"From the kindness of your speech, and from the very polite welcome given me by your household, I imagine that you have not always been a woodcutter. Perhaps you formerly belonged to one of the upper classes?"

Smiling, the woodcutter answered:

[1]A sort of little fireplace, contrived in the floor of a room, is thus described. The *ro* is usually a square shallow cavity, lined with metal and half-filled with ashes, in which charcoal is lighted.

"Sir, you are not mistaken. Though now living as you find me, I was once a person of some distinction. My story is the story of a ruined life—ruined by my own fault. I used to be in the service of a daimyō; and my rank in that service was not inconsiderable. But I loved women and wine too well; and under the influence of passion I acted wickedly. My selfishness brought about the ruin of our house, and caused the death of many persons. Retribution followed me; and I long remained a fugitive in the land. Now I often pray that I may be able to make some atonement for the evil which I did, and to reëstablish the ancestral home. But I fear that I shall never find any way of so doing. Nevertheless, I try to overcome the karma of my errors by sincere repentance, and by helping, as far as I can, those who are unfortunate."

Kwairyō was pleased by this announcement of good resolve; and he said to the *aruji:*

"My friend, I have had occasion to observe that men, prone to folly in their youth, may in after years become very earnest in right living. In the holy sûtras it is written that those strongest in wrong-doing can become, by power of good resolve, the strongest in right-doing. I do not doubt that you have a good heart; and I hope that better fortune will come to you. To-night I shall recite the sûtras for your sake, and pray that you may obtain the force to overcome the karma of any past errors."

With these assurances, Kwairyō bade the *aruji* good-night; and his host showed him to a very small side-room, where a bed had been made ready. Then all went to sleep except the priest, who began to read the sûtras by the light of a paper lantern. Until a late hour he continued to read and pray: then he opened a window in his little sleeping-room, to take a last look at the landscape before lying down. The night was beautiful: there was no cloud in the sky; there was no wind; and the strong moonlight threw down sharp black shadows of foliage, and glittered on the dews of the garden. Shrillings of crickets and bell-insects made a musical tumult; and the sound of the neighboring cascade deepened with the night. Kwairyō felt thirsty as he listened to the noise of the water; and, remembering the bamboo aqueduct at the rear of the house, he thought that he could go there and get a drink without disturbing the sleeping household. Very gently he pushed apart the sliding-screens that separated his room from the main apartment; and he saw, by the light of the lantern, five recumbent bodies—without heads!

For one instant he stood bewildered,—imagining a crime. But in another moment he perceived that there was no blood, and that the headless necks did not look as if they had been cut. Then he thought to himself: "Either this is an illusion made by goblins, or I have been lured into the dwelling of a Rokuro-Kubi. . . . In the book *Sōshinki* it is written that if one find the body of a Rokuro-Kubi without its head, and remove the body to another place, the head will never be able to join itself again to the neck. And the book further says that when the head comes back and finds that its body has been moved, it will strike itself upon the floor three times—bounding like a ball—and will pant as in great fear, and presently die. Now, if these be Rokuro-Kubi, they mean me no good—so I shall be justified in following the instructions of the book." . . .

He seized the body of the *aruji* by the feet, pulled it to the window, and pushed it out. Then he went to the back-door, which he found barred; and he surmised that the heads had made their exit through the smoke-hole in the roof, which had been left open. Gently unbarring the door, he made his way to the garden, and proceeded with all possible caution to the grove beyond it. He heard voices talking in the grove; and he went in the direction of the voices—stealing from shadow to shadow, until he reached a good hiding-place. Then, from behind a trunk, he caught sight of the heads—all five of them—flitting about, and chatting as they flitted. They were eating worms and insects which they found on the ground or among the trees. Presently the head of the *aruji* stopped eating and said:

"Ah, the traveling priest who came to-night!—how fat all his body is! When we shall have eaten him, our bellies will be well filled. . . . I was foolish to talk to him as I did;—it only set him to reciting the sûtras on behalf of my soul! To go near him while he is reciting would be difficult; and we cannot touch him so long as he is praying. But as it is now nearly morning, perhaps he has gone to sleep.... Some one of you go to the house and see what the fellow is doing."

Another head—the head of a young woman—immediately rose up and flitted to the house, lightly as a bat. After a few minutes it came back, and cried out huskily, in a tone of great alarm:

"That traveling priest is not in the house; he is gone! But that is not the worst of the matter. He has taken the body of our *aruji;* and I do not know where he has put it."

At this announcement the head of the *aruji*—distinctly visible in the moonlight—assumed a frightful aspect: its eyes opened monstrously; its hair stood up bristling; and its teeth gnashed. Then a cry burst from its lips; and—weeping tears of rage—it exclaimed:

"Since my body has been moved, to rejoin it is not possible! Then I must die!... And all through the work of that priest! Before I die I will get at that priest!—I will tear him!—I will devour him!... *And there he is*—behind that tree!—hiding behind that tree! See him!—the fat coward!"...

In the same moment the head of the *aruji*, followed by the other four heads, sprang at Kwairyō. But the strong priest had already armed himself by plucking up a young tree; and with that tree he struck the heads as they came—knocking them from him with tremendous blows. Four of them fled away. But the head of the *aruji*, though battered again and again, desperately continued to bound at the priest, and at last caught him by the left sleeve of his robe. Kwairyō, however, as quickly gripped the head by its topknot, and repeatedly struck it. It did not release its hold; but it uttered a long moan, and thereafter ceased to struggle. It was dead. But its teeth still held the sleeve; and, for all his great strength, Kwairyō could not force open the jaws.

With the head still hanging to his sleeve he went back to the house, and there caught sight of the other four Rokuro-Kubi squatting together, with their bruised and bleeding heads reunited to their bodies. But when they perceived him at the back-door all screamed, "The priest! the priest!"—and fled, through the other doorway, out into the woods.

Eastward the sky was brightening; day was about to dawn; and Kwairyō knew that the power of the goblins was limited to the hours of darkness. He looked at the head clinging to his sleeve—its face all fouled with blood and foam and clay; and he laughed aloud as he thought to himself: "What a *miyagé!*[1]—the head of a goblin!" After which he gathered together his few belongings, and leisurely descended the mountain to continue his journey.

Right on he journeyed, until he came to Suwa in Shinano; and into the main street of Suwa he solemnly strode, with the head dangling at his elbow. Then women fainted, and children screamed and ran away; and there was a great crowding and clamoring until the *torité* (as the police of those days were called) seized the priest, and took him to jail. For they supposed the head to be the head of a murdered man who, in the moment of being killed, had caught the murderer's sleeve in his teeth. As for Kwairyō, he only smiled and said nothing when they questioned him. So, after having passed a night in prison, he was brought before the magistrates of the district. Then he was ordered to explain how he, a priest, had been found with the head of a man fastened to his sleeve, and why he had dared thus shamelessly to parade his crime in the sight of the people.

Kwairyō laughed long and loudly at these questions; and then he said:

"Sirs, I did not fasten the head to my sleeve: it fastened itself there—much against my will. And I have not committed any crime. For this is not the head of a man; it is the head of a goblin; and, if I caused the death of the goblin, I did not do so by any shedding of blood, but simply by taking the precautions necessary to assure my own safety." . . . And he proceeded to relate the whole of the adventure—bursting into another hearty laugh as he told of his encounter with the five heads.

But the magistrates did not laugh. They judged him to be a hardened criminal, and his story an insult to their intelligence.

[1]A present made to friends or to the household on returning from a journey is thus called. Ordinarily, of course, the *miyagé* consists of something produced in the locality to which the journey has been made: this is the point of Kwairyō's jest.

Therefore, without further questioning, they decided to order his immediate execution—all of them except one, a very old man. This aged officer had made no remark during the trial; but, after having heard the opinion of his colleagues, he rose up, and said:

"Let us first examine the head carefully; for this, I think, has not yet been done. If the priest has spoken truth, the head itself should bear witness for him . . . Bring the head here!"

So the head, still holding in its teeth the *koromo* that had been stripped from Kwairyō's shoulders, was put before the judges. The old man turned it round and round, carefully examined it, and discovered, on the nape of its neck, several strange red characters. He called the attention of his colleagues to these, and also bade them observe that the edges of the neck nowhere presented the appearance of having been cut by any weapon. On the contrary, the line of severance was smooth as the line at which a falling leaf detaches itself from the stem . . . Then said the elder:

"I am quite sure that the priest told us nothing but the truth. This is the head of a Rokuro-Kubi. In the book *Ńan-hō-ï-butsu-shi* it is written that certain red characters can always be found upon the nape of the neck of a real Rokuro-Kubi. There are the characters: you can see for yourselves that they have not been painted. Moreover, it is well known that such goblins have been dwelling in the mountains of the province of Kai from very ancient time. . . . But you, Sir," he exclaimed, turning to Kwairyō—"what sort of sturdy priest may you be? Certainly you have given proof of a courage that few priests possess; and you have the air of a soldier rather than of a priest. Perhaps you once belonged to the samurai-class?"

"You have guessed rightly, Sir," Kwairyō responded. "Before becoming a priest, I long followed the profession of arms; and in those days I never feared man or devil. My name then was Isogai Héïdazaëmon Takétsura, of Kyūshū: there may be some among you who remember it."

At the utterance of that name, a murmur of admiration filled the court-room; for there were many present who remembered it. And Kwairyō immediately found himself among friends instead of judges—friends anxious to prove their admiration by fraternal kindness. With honor they escorted him to the residence of the daimyō, who welcomed him, and feasted him, and made him a handsome present before allowing him to depart. When Kwairyō left Suwa, he was as happy as any priest is permitted to be in this transitory world. As for the head, he took it with him,—jocosely insisting that he intended it for a *miyagé*.

And now it only remains to tell what became of the head.

A day or two after leaving Suwa, Kwairyō met with a robber, who stopped him in a lonesome place, and bade him strip. Kwairyō at once removed his *koromo,* and offered it to the robber, who then first perceived what was hanging to the sleeve. Though brave, the highwayman was startled: he dropped the garment, and sprang back. Then he cried out:—"You!—what kind of a priest are you? Why, you are a worse man than I am! It is true that I have killed people; but I never walked about with anybody's head fastened to my sleeve. . . . Well, Sir priest, I suppose we are of the same calling; and I must say that I admire you! . . . Now that head would be of use to me: I could frighten people with it. Will you sell it? You can have my robe in exchange for your *koromo;* and I will give you five ryō for the head."

Kwairyō answered:—

"I shall let you have the head and the robe if you insist; but I must tell you that this is not the head of a man. It is a goblin's head. So, if you buy it, and have any trouble in consequence, please to remember that you were not deceived by me."

"What a nice priest you are!" exclaimed the robber. "You kill men, and jest about it! . . . But I am really in earnest. Here is my robe; and here is the money—and let me have the head. . . . What is the use of joking?"

"Take the thing," said Kwairyō. "I was not joking. The only joke—if there be any joke at all—is that you are fool enough to pay good money for a goblin's head." And Kwairyō, loudly laughing, went upon his way.

Thus the robber got the head and the *koromo;* and for some time he played goblin-priest upon the highways. But, reaching the neighborhood of Suwa, he there learned the real history of the head; and he then became afraid that the spirit of the Rokuro-Kubi might give him trouble. So he made up his mind to take back the head to the place from which it had come, and to bury it with its body. He found his way to the lonely cottage in the mountains of Kai; but nobody was there, and he could not discover the body. Therefore he buried the head by itself, in the grove behind the cottage; and he had a tombstone set up over the grave; and he caused a Ségaki-service to be performed on behalf of the spirit of the Rokuro-Kubi. And that tombstone —known as the Tombstone of the Rokuro-Kubi—may be seen (at least so the Japanese story-teller declares) even unto this day.

A DEAD SECRET

A Dead Secret

A Dead Secret

A long time ago, in the province of Tamba, there lived a rich merchant named Inamuraya Gensuké. He had a daughter called O-Sono. As she was very clever and pretty, he thought it would be a pity to let her grow up with only such teaching as the country-teachers could give her: so he sent her, in care of some trusty attendants, to Kyōto, that she might be trained in the polite accomplishments taught to the ladies of the capital. After she had thus been educated, she was married to a friend of her father's family—a merchant named Nagaraya—and she lived happily with him for nearly four years. They had one child—a boy. But O-Sono fell ill and died in the fourth year after her marriage.

On the night after the funeral of O-Sono, her little son said that his mamma had come back, and was in the room upstairs. She had smiled at him, but would not talk to him: so he became afraid, and ran away. Then some of the family went upstairs to the room which had been O-Sono's; and they were startled to see, by the light of a small lamp which had been kindled before a shrine in that room, the figure of the dead mother. She appeared as if standing in front of a *tansu,* or chest of drawers, that still contained her ornaments and her wearing-apparel. Her head and shoulders could be very distinctly seen; but from the waist downward the figure thinned into invisibility—and it was like an imperfect reflection of her, and transparent as a shadow on water.

Then the folk were afraid, and left the room. Below they consulted together; and the mother of O-Sono's husband said: "A woman is fond of her small things; and O-Sono was much attached to her belongings. Perhaps she has come back to look at them. Many dead persons will do that—unless the things be given to the parish-temple. If we present O-Sono's robes and girdles to the temple, her spirit will probably find rest."

It was agreed that this should be done as soon as possible. So on the following morning the drawers were emptied; and all of O-Sono's ornaments and dresses were taken to the temple. But she came back the next night, and looked at the *tansu* as before. And she came back also on the night following, and the night after that, and every night—and the house became a house of fear.

The mother of O-Sono's husband then went to the parish-temple, and told the chief priest all that had happened, and asked for ghostly counsel. The temple was a Zen temple; and the head-priest was a learned old man, known as Daigen Oshō. He said: "There must be something about which she is anxious, in or near that *tansu*." "But we emptied all the drawers," replied the old woman; "there is nothing in the *tansu*." "Well," said Daigen Oshō, "to-night I shall go to your house, and keep watch in that room, and see what can be done. You must give orders that no person shall enter the room while I am watching, unless I call."

After sundown, Daigen-Oshō went to the house, and found the room made ready for him. He remained there alone, reading the sûtras; and nothing appeared until after the Hour of the Rat.[1] Then the figure of O-Sono outlined itself in front of the *tansu*. Her face had a wistful look; and she kept her eyes fixed upon the *tansu*.

The priest uttered the holy formula prescribed in such

[1]The Hour of the Rat *(Né-no-Koku)*, according to the old Japanese method of reckoning time, was the first hour. It corresponded to the time between our midnight and two o'clock in the morning; for the ancient Japanese hours were each equal to two modern hours.

cases, and then, addressing the figure by the *kaimyō*[2] of O-Sono, said: "I have come here in order to help you. Perhaps in that *tansu* there is something about which you have reason to feel anxious. Shall I try to find it for you?" The shadow appeared to give assent by a slight motion of the head; and the priest, rising, opened the top drawer. It was empty. Successively he opened the second, the third, and the fourth drawer; he searched carefully behind them and beneath them; he carefully examined the interior of the chest. He found nothing. But the figure remained gazing as wistfully as before. "What can she want?" thought the priest. Suddenly it occurred to him that there might be something hidden under the paper with which the drawers were lined. He removed the lining of the first drawer:—nothing! He removed the lining of the second and third drawers:—still nothing. But under the lining of the lowermost drawer he found—a letter. "Is this the thing about which you have been troubled?" he asked. The shadow of the woman turned toward him,—her faint gaze fixed upon the letter. "Shall I burn it for you?" he asked. She bowed before him. "It shall be burned in the temple this very morning," he promised—"and no one shall read it, except myself." The figure smiled and vanished.

Dawn was breaking as the priest descended the stairs, to find the family waiting anxiously below. "Do not be anxious," he said to them: "she will not appear again." And she never did.

The letter was burned. It was a love-letter written to O-Sono in the time of her studies at Kyōto. But the priest alone knew what was in it; and the secret died with him.

[2]*Kaimyō*, the posthumous Buddhist name, or religious name, given to the dead. Strictly speaking, the meaning of the word is silâ-name. (See my paper entitled "The Literature of the Dead" in *Exotics and Retrospectives.*)

YUKI-ONNA

Yuki-Onna

Yuki-Onna

In a village of Musashi Province, there lived two woodcutters: Mosaku and Minokichi. At the time of which I am speaking, Mosaku was an old man; and Minokichi, his apprentice, was a lad of eighteen years. Every day they went together to a forest situated about five miles from their village. On the way to that forest there is a wide river to cross; and there is a ferryboat. Several times a bridge was built where the ferry is; but the bridge was each time carried away by a flood. No common bridge can resist the current there when the river rises.

Mosaku and Minokichi were on their way home, one very cold evening, when a great snowstorm overtook them. They reached the ferry; and they found that the boatman had gone away, leaving his boat on the other side of the river. It was no day for swimming; and the woodcutters took shelter in the ferryman's hut—thinking themselves lucky to find any shelter at all. There was no brazier in the hut, nor any place in which to make a fire: it was only a two-mat[1] hut, with a single door, but no window. Mosaku and Minokichi fastened the door, and lay down to rest, with their straw raincoats over them. At first they did not feel very cold; and they thought that the storm would soon be over.

The old man almost immediately fell asleep; but the boy,

[1] That is to say, with a floor-surface of about six feet square.

Minokichi, lay awake a long time, listening to the awful wind, and the continual slashing of the snow against the door. The river was roaring; and the hut swayed and creaked like a junk at sea. It was a terrible storm; and the air was every moment becoming colder; and Minokichi shivered under his raincoat. But at last, in spite of the cold, he too fell asleep.

He was awakened by a showering of snow in his face. The door of the hut had been forced open; and, by the snow-light *(yuki-akari)*, he saw a woman in the room—a woman all in white. She was bending above Mosaku, and blowing her breath upon him—and her breath was like a bright white smoke. Almost in the same moment she turned to Minokichi, and stooped over him. He tried to cry out, but found that he could not utter any sound. The white woman bent down over him, lower and lower, until her face almost touched him; and he saw that she was very beautiful,—though her eyes made him afraid. For a little time she continued to look at him; then she smiled, and she whispered: "I intended to treat you like the other man. But I cannot help feeling some pity for you, because you are so young. . . . You are a pretty boy, Minokichi; and I will not hurt you now. But, if you ever tell anybody—even your own mother—about what you have seen this night, I shall know it; and then I will kill you. . . . Remember what I say!"

With these words, she turned from him and passed through the doorway. Then he found himself able to move; and he sprang up, and looked out. But the woman was nowhere to be seen; and the snow was driving furiously into the hut. Minokichi closed the door, and secured it by fixing several billets of wood against it. He wondered if the wind had blown it open; he thought that he might have been only dreaming, and might have mistaken the gleam of the snow-light in the doorway for the figure of a white woman: but he could not be sure. He called to Mosaku, and was frightened because the old man did not answer. He put out his hand in the dark, and touched Mosaku's face, and found that it was ice! Mosaku was stark and dead. . . .

By dawn the storm was over; and when the ferryman returned to his station, a little after sunrise, he found Minokichi lying senseless beside the frozen body of Mosaku. Minokichi was promptly cared for, and soon came to himself; but he remained a long time ill from the effects of the cold of that terrible night. He had been greatly frightened also by the old man's death; but he said nothing about the vision of the woman in white. As soon as he got well again, he returned to his calling—going alone every morning to the forest, and coming back at nightfall with his bundles of wood, which his mother helped him to sell.

One evening, in the winter of the following year, as he was on his way home, he overtook a girl who happened to be traveling by the same road. She was a tall, slim girl, very good-looking; and she answered Minokichi's greeting in a voice as pleasant to the ear as the voice of a song-bird. Then he walked beside her; and they began to talk. The girl said that her name was O-Yuki;[1] that she had lately lost both of her parents; and that she was going to Yedo, where she happened to have some poor relations, who might help her to find a situation as servant. Minokichi soon felt charmed by this strange girl; and the more that he looked at her, the handsomer she appeared to be. He asked her whether she was yet betrothed; and she answered, laughingly, that she was free. Then, in her turn, she asked Minokichi whether he was married, or pledged to marry; and he told her that, although he had only a widowed mother to support, the question of an "honorable daughter-in-law" had not yet been considered, as he was very young. . . . After these confidences, they walked on for a long while without speaking; but, as the proverb declares, *Ki ga aréba, mé mo kuchi hodo ni mono wo iu:* "When the wish is there, the eyes can say as much as the mouth." By the time they reached the village, they had become very much pleased with each other; and then Minokichi asked O-Yuki to rest awhile at his house. After some shy hesitation, she went there with him; and his mother made her welcome, and prepared a warm meal for her. O-Yuki behaved so nicely that Minokichi's mother took a sudden fancy to her, and

[1] This name, signifying "Snow", is not uncommon. On the subject of Japanese female names, see my paper in the volume entitled *Shadowings.*

persuaded her to delay her journey to Yedo. And the natural end of the matter was that Yuki never went to Yedo at all. She remained in the house, as an "honorable daughter-in-law".

O-Yuki proved a very good daughter-in-law. When Minokichi's mother came to die,—some five years later—her last words were words of affection and praise for the wife of her son. And O-Yuki bore Minokichi ten children, boys and girls—handsome children all of them, and very fair of skin.

The country-folk thought O-Yuki a wonderful person, by nature different from themselves. Most of the peasant-women age early; but O-Yuki, even after having become the mother of ten children, looked as young and fresh as on the day when she had first come to the village.

One night, after the children had gone to sleep, O-Yuki was sewing by the light of a paper lamp; and Minokichi, watching her, said:—

"To see you sewing there, with the light on your face, makes me think of a strange thing that happened when I was a lad of eighteen. I then saw somebody as beautiful and white as you are now—indeed, she was very like you." ...

Without lifting her eyes from her work, O-Yuki responded:—

"Tell me about her. ... Where did you see her?"

Then Minokichi told her about the terrible night in the ferryman's hut—and about the White Woman that had stooped above him, smiling and whispering—and about the silent death of old Mosaku. And he said:

"Asleep or awake, that was the only time that I saw a being as beautiful as you. Of course, she was not a human being; and I was afraid of her—very much afraid—but she was so white! ... Indeed, I have never been sure whether it was a dream that I saw, or the Woman of the Snow." ...

O-Yuki flung down her sewing, and arose, and bowed above Minokichi where he sat, and shrieked into his face:

"It was I—I—I! Yuki it was! And I told you then that I would kill you if you ever said one word about it! ... But for those children asleep there, I would kill you this moment! And now you had better take very, very good care of them; for if ever they have reason to complain of you, I will treat you as you deserve!" . . .

Even as she screamed, her voice came thin, like a crying of wind; then she melted into a bright white mist that spired to the roof-beams, and shuddered away through the smoke-hole. . . . Never again was she seen.

THE STORY OF AOYAGI

The Story of Aoyagi

The Story of Aoyagi

In the era of Bummei [1469–1486] there was a young samurai called Tomotada in the service of Hatakéyama Yoshimuné, the Lord of Noto. Tomotada was a native of Echizen; but at an early age he had been taken, as page, into the palace of the daimyō of Noto, and had been educated, under the supervision of that prince, for the profession of arms. As he grew up, he proved himself both a good scholar and a good soldier, and continued to enjoy the favor of his prince. Being gifted with an amiable character, a winning address, and a very handsome person, he was admired and much liked by his samurai-comrades.

When Tomotada was about twenty years old, he was sent upon a private mission to Hosokawa Masamoto, the great daimyō of Kyōto, a kinsman of Hatakéyama Yoshimuné. Having been ordered to journey through Echizen, the youth requested and obtained permission to pay a visit, on the way, to his widowed mother.

It was the coldest period of the year when he started; the country was covered with snow; and, though mounted upon a powerful horse, he found himself obliged to proceed slowly. The road which he followed passed through a mountain-district where the settlements were few and far between; and on the second day of his journey, after a weary ride of hours, he was dismayed to find that he could not reach his intended halting-place until late in the night. He had reason to be anxious

—for a heavy snowstorm came on, with an intensely cold wind; and the horse showed signs of exhaustion. But, in that trying moment, Tomotada unexpectedly perceived the thatched roof of a cottage on the summit of a near hill, where willow-trees were growing. With difficulty he urged his tired animal to the dwelling; and he loudly knocked upon the storm-doors, which had been closed against the wind. An old woman opened them, and cried out compassionately at the sight of the handsome stranger: "Ah, how pitiful!—a young gentleman traveling alone in such weather! . . . Deign, young master, to enter."

Tomotada dismounted, and after leading his horse to a shed in the rear, entered the cottage, where he saw an old man and a girl warming themselves by a fire of bamboo splints. They respectfully invited him to approach the fire; and the old folks then proceeded to warm some rice-wine, and to prepare food for the traveler, whom they ventured to question in regard to his journey. Meanwhile the young girl disappeared behind a screen. Tomatoda had observed, with astonishment, that she was extremely beautiful—though her attire was of the most wretched kind, and her long, loose hair in disorder. He wondered that so handsome a girl should be living in such a miserable and lonesome place.

The old man said to him:

"Honored Sir, the next village is far; and the snow is falling thickly. The wind is piercing; and the road is very bad. Therefore, to proceed further this night would probably be dangerous. Although this hovel is unworthy of your presence, and although we have not any comfort to offer, perhaps it were safer to remain to-night under this miserable roof. . . . We would take good care of your horse."

Tomotada accepted this humble proposal—secretly glad of the chance thus afforded him to see more of the young girl. Presently a coarse but ample meal was set before him; and the girl came from behind the screen, to serve the wine. She was now reclad, in a rough but cleanly robe of homespun; and her long, loose hair had been neatly combed and smoothed. As she bent forward to fill his cup, Tomatoda was amazed to perceive that she was incomparably more beautiful than any woman whom he had ever before seen; and there was a grace about her every motion that astonished him. But the elders began to apologize for her, saying: "Sir, our daughter, Aoyagi,[1] has been brought up here, in the mountains, almost alone; and she knows nothing of gentle service. We pray that you will pardon her stupidity and her ignorance." Tomotada protested that he deemed himself lucky to be waited upon by so comely a maiden. He could not turn his eyes away from her—though he saw that his admiring gaze made her blush—and he left the wine and food untasted before him. The mother said: "Kind Sir, we very much hope that you will try to eat and to drink a little—though our peasant-fare is of the worst—as you must have been chilled by that piercing wind." Then, to please the old folks, Tomotada ate and drank as he could; but the charm of the blushing girl still grew upon him. He talked with her, and found that her speech was sweet as her face. Brought up in the mountains she might have been; but, in that case, her parents must at some time have been persons of high degree; for she spoke and moved like a damsel of rank. Suddenly he addressed her with a poem—which was also a question—inspired by the delight in his heart:

"Tadzunétsuru,
Hana ka toté koso,
Hi wo kurasé,
Akénu ni otoru
Akané sasuran?"

[*Being on my way to pay a visit, I found that which I took to be a flower: therefore here I spend the day . . . Why, in the time before dawn, the dawn-blush tint should glow—that, indeed, I know not.*"][2]

[1]The name signifies "Green Willow";—though rarely met with, it is still in use.

[2]The poem may be read in two ways; several of the phrases having a double meaning. But the art of its construction would need considerable space to explain, and could scarcely interest the Western reader. The meaning which Tomotada desired to convey might be thus expressed:—"While journeying to visit my mother, I met with a being lovely as a flower; and for the sake of that lovely person, I am passing the day here. . . . Fair one, wherefore that dawn-like blush before the hour of dawn?—can it mean that you love me?"

Without a moment's hesitation, she answered him in these verses: —

"Izuru hi no
Honoméku iro wo
Waga sodé ni
Tsutsumaba asu mo
Kimiya tomaran."

[*"If with my sleeve I hide the faint fair color of the dawning sun — then, perhaps, in the morning my lord will remain."*][1]

Then Tomotada knew that she accepted his admiration; and he was scarcely less surprised by the art with which she had uttered her feelings in verse, than delighted by the assurance which the verses conveyed. He was now certain that in all this world he could not hope to meet, much less to win, a girl more beautiful and witty than this rustic maid before him; and a voice in his heart seemed to cry out urgently: "Take the luck that the gods have put in your way!" In short he was bewitched — bewitched to such a degree that, without further preliminary, he asked the old people to give him their daughter in marriage — telling them, at the same time, his name and lineage, and his rank in the train of the Lord of Noto.

They bowed down before him with many exclamations of grateful astonishment. But after some moments of apparent hesitation the father replied:

"Honored master, you are a person of high position, and likely to rise to still higher things. Too great is the favor that you deign to offer us; indeed, the depth of our gratitude therefor is not to be spoken or measured. But this girl of ours, being a stupid country-girl of vulgar birth, with no training or teaching of any sort, it would be improper to let her become the wife of a noble samurai. Even to speak of such a matter is not right. . . . But, since you find the girl to your liking, and have condescended to pardon her peasant-manners and to overlook her great rudeness, we do gladly present her to you, for an humble

[1] Another reading is possible; but this one gives the signification of the *answer* intended.

handmaid. Deign, therefore, to act hereafter in her regard according to your august pleasure."

Ere morning the storm had passed; and day broke through a cloudless east. Even if the sleeve of Aoyagi hid from her lover's eyes the rose-blush of that dawn, he could no longer tarry. But neither could he resign himself to part with the girl; and, when everything had been prepared for his journey, he thus addressed her parents:

"Though it may seem thankless to ask for more than I have already received, I must once again beg you to give me your daughter for wife. It would be difficult for me to separate from her now; and as she is willing to accompany me, if you permit, I can take her with me as she is. If you will give her to me, I shall ever cherish you as parents. . . . And, in the meantime, please to accept this poor acknowledgment of your kindest hospitality."

So saying, he placed before his humble host a purse of gold *ryō*. But the old man, after many prostrations, gently pushed back the gift, and said:

"Kind master, the gold would be of no use to us; and you will probably have need of it during your long, cold journey. Here we buy nothing; and we could not spend so much money upon ourselves, even if we wished. . . . As for the girl, we have already bestowed her as a free gift—she belongs to you: therefore it is not necessary to ask our leave to take her away. Already she has told us that she hopes to accompany you, and to remain your servant so long as you may be willing to endure her presence. We are only too happy to know that you deign to accept her; and we pray that you will not trouble yourself on our account. In this place we could not provide her with proper clothing—much less with a dowry. Moreover, being old, we should in any event have to separate from her before long. Therefore it is very fortunate that you should be willing to take her with you now."

It was in vain that Tomotada tried to persuade the old people to accept a present: he found that they cared nothing for money. But he saw that they were really anxious to trust their daughter's fate to his hands; and he therefore decided to take her with him. So he placed her upon his horse, and bade the old folks farewell for the time being, with many sincere expressions of gratitude.

"Honored Sir," the father made answer, "it is we, and not you, who have reason for gratitude. We are sure that you will be kind to our girl; and we have no fears for her sake." . . .

[*Here, in the Japanese original, there is a queer break in the natural course of the narration, which therefrom remains curiously inconsistent. Nothing further is said about the mother of Tomotada, or about the parents of Aoyagi, or about the daimyō of Noto. Evidently the writer wearied of his work at this point, and hurried the story, very carelessly, to its startling end. I am not able to supply his omissions, or to repair his faults of construction; but I must venture to put in a few explanatory details, without which the rest of the tale would not hold together. . . . It appears that Tomotada rashly took Aoyagi with him to Kyōto, and so got into trouble; but we are not informed as to where the couple lived afterwards.*]

. . . Now a samurai was not allowed to marry without the consent of his lord; and Tomotada could not expect to obtain this sanction before his mission had been accomplished. He had reason, under such circumstances, to fear that the beauty of Aoyagi might attract dangerous attention, and that means might be devised of taking her away from him. In Kyōto he therefore tried to keep her hidden from curious eyes. But a retainer of the Lord Hosokawa one day caught sight of Aoyagi, discovered her relation to Tomotada, and reported the matter to the daimyō. Thereupon the daimyō—a young prince, and fond of pretty faces—gave orders that the girl should be brought to the palace; and she was taken thither at once, without ceremony.

Tomotada sorrowed unspeakably; but he knew himself powerless. He was only an humble messenger in the service of a far-off daimyō; and for the time being he was at the mercy of a much more powerful daimyō, whose wishes were not to be questioned. Moreover Tomatoda knew that he had acted foolishly—that he had brought about his own misfortune, by entering into a clandestine relation which the code of the military class condemned. There was now but one hope for him—a desperate hope: that Aoyagi might be able and willing to escape and to flee with him. After long reflection, he resolved to try to send her a letter. The attempt would be dangerous, of course: any writing sent to her might find its way to the hands of the daïmyō; and to send a love-letter to any inmate of the palace was an unpardonable offense. But he resolved to dare the risk; and, in the form of a Chinese poem, he composed a letter which he endeavored to have conveyed to her. The poem was written with only twenty-eight characters. But with those twenty-eight characters he was able to express all the depth of his passion, and to suggest all the pain of his loss:[1]

Kōshi ō-son gojin wo ou;
Ryokuju namida wo tarété rakin wo hitataru;
Komon hitotabi irité fukaki koto umi no gotoshi;
Koré yori shorō koré rojin.

[*Closely, closely the youthful prince now follows after the gem-bright maid;—*

The tears of the fair one, falling, have moistened all her robes.

But the august lord, having once become enamored of her—the depth of his longing is like the depth of the sea.

Therefore it is only I that am left forlorn,—only I that am left to wander alone.]

On the evening of the day after this poem had been sent, Tomotada was summoned to appear before the Lord Hosokawa. The youth at once suspected that his confidence had been betrayed; and he could not hope, if his letter had been seen by the daimyō, to escape the severest penalty. "Now he will order my death," thought Tomotada; "but I do not care to live unless Aoyagi be restored to me. Besides, if the death-sentence be passed, I can at least try to kill Hosokawa." He slipped his swords into his girdle, and hastened to the palace.

[1] So the Japanese story-teller would have us believe—although the verses seem commonplace in translation. I have tried to give only their general meaning: an effective literal translation would require some scholarship.

On entering the presence-room he saw the Lord Hosokawa seated upon the daïs, surrounded by samurai of high rank, in caps and robes of ceremony. All were silent as statues; and while Tomotada advanced to make obeisance, the hush seemed to him sinister and heavy, like the stillness before a storm. But Hosokawa suddenly descended from the daïs, and, taking the youth by the arm, began to repeat the words of the poem;—"*Kōshi ō-son gojin wo ou.*" . . . And Tomotada, looking up, saw kindly tears in the prince's eyes.

Then said Hosokawa:

"Because you love each other so much, I have taken it upon myself to authorize your marriage, in lieu of my kinsman, the Lord of Noto; and your wedding shall now be celebrated before me. The guests are assembled;—the gifts are ready."

At a signal from the lord, the sliding-screens concealing a further apartment were pushed open; and Tomotada saw there many dignitaries of the court, assembled for the ceremony, and Aoyagi awaiting him in bride's apparel. . . . Thus was she given back to him; and the wedding was joyous and splendid; and precious gifts were made to the young couple by the prince, and by the members of his household.

*

* *

For five happy years, after that wedding, Tomotada and Aoyagi dwelt together. But one morning Aoyagi, while talking with her husband about some household matter, suddenly uttered a great cry of pain, and then became very white and still. After a few moments she said, in a feeble voice: "Pardon me for thus rudely crying out—but the pain was so sudden! . . . My dear husband, our union must have been brought about through some Karma-relation in a former state of existence; and that happy relation, I think, will bring us again together in more than one life to come. But for this present existence of ours, the relation is now ended—we are about to be separated. Repeat for me, I beseech you, the *Nembutsu*-prayer—because I am dying."

"Oh! what strange wild fancies!" cried the startled husband—"you are only a little unwell, my dear one! . . . lie down for a while, and rest; and the sickness will pass." . . .

"No, no!" she responded—"I am dying!—I do not imagine it;—I know! . . . And it were needless now, my dear husband, to hide the truth from you any longer: I am not a human being. The soul of a tree is my soul; the heart of a tree is my heart; the sap of the willow is my life. And some one, at this cruel moment, is cutting down my tree; that is why I must die! . . . Even to weep were now beyond my strength!—quickly, quickly, repeat the *Nembutsu* for me . . . quickly! . . . Ah!" . . .

With another cry of pain she turned aside her beautiful head, and tried to hide her face behind her sleeve. But almost in the same moment her whole form appeared to collapse in the strangest way, and to sink down, down, down—level with the floor. Tomotada had sprung to support her; but there was nothing to support! There lay on the matting only the empty robes of the fair creature and the ornaments that she had worn in her hair: the body had ceased to exist. . . .

Tomotada shaved his head, took the Buddhist vows, and became an itinerant priest. He traveled through all the provinces of the empire; and, at all the holy places which he visited, he offered up prayers for the soul of Aoyagi. Reaching Echizen, in the course of his pilgrimage, he sought the home of the parents of his beloved. But when he arrived at the lonely place among the hills, where their dwelling had been, he found that the cottage had disappeared. There was nothing to mark even the spot where it had stood, except the stumps of three willows—two old trees and one young tree—that had been cut down long before his arrival.

Beside the stumps of those willow-trees he erected a memorial tomb, inscribed with divers holy texts; and he there performed many Buddhist services on behalf of the spirits of Aoyagi and of her parents.

JIU-ROKU-
ZAKURA

Jiu-Roku-Zakura

Jiu-Roku-Zakura

Uso no yona—
Jiu-roku-zakura
Saki ni keri!

In Wakégōri, a district of the province of Iyo, there is a very ancient and famous cherry-tree, called *Jiu-roku-zakura,* or "the Cherry-tree of the Sixteenth Day", because it blooms every year upon the sixteenth day of the first month (by the old lunar calendar)—and only upon that day. Thus the time of its flowering is the Period of Great Cold—though the natural habit of a cherry-tree is to wait for the spring season before venturing to blossom. But the *Jiu-roku-zakura* blossoms with a life that is not—or, at least, was not originally—its own. There is the ghost of a man in that tree.

He was a samurai of Iyo; and the tree grew in his garden; and it used to flower at the usual time—that is to say, about the end of March or the beginning of April. He had played under that tree when he was a child; and his parents and grandparents and ancestors had hung to its blossoming branches, season after season for more than a hundred years, bright strips of colored paper inscribed with poems of praise. He himself became very old—outliving all his children; and there was nothing in the world left for him to love except that tree. And lo! in the summer of a certain year, the tree withered and died!

Exceedingly the old man sorrowed for his tree. Then kind neighbors found for him a young and beautiful cherry-tree, and planted it in his garden—hoping thus to comfort him. And he thanked them, and pretended to be glad. But really his heart was full of pain; for he had loved the old tree so well that nothing could have consoled him for the loss of it.

At last there came to him a happy thought: he remembered a way by which the perishing tree might be saved. (It was the sixteenth day of the first month.) Alone he went into his garden, and bowed down before the withered tree, and spoke to it, saying: "Now deign, I beseech you, once more to bloom—because I am going to die in your stead." (For it is believed that one can really give away one's life to another person, or to a creature, or even to a tree, by the favor of the gods—and thus to transfer one's life is expressed by the term *migawari ni tatsu,* "to act as a substitute".) Then under that tree he spread a white cloth, and divers coverings, and sat down upon the coverings, and performed *hari-kiri* after the fashion of a samurai. And the ghost of him went into the tree, and made it blossom in that same hour.

And every year it still blooms on the sixteenth day of the first month, in the season of snow.

THE DREAM OF AKINOSUKÉ

The Dream of Akinosuké

The Dream of Akinosuké

In the district called Toïchi of Yamato province, there used to live a gōshi named Miyata Akinosuké. . . . [Here I must tell you that in Japanese feudal times there was a privileged class of soldier-farmers—free-holders—corresponding to the class of yeomen in England; and these were called gōshi.]

In Akinosuké's garden there was a great and ancient cedar-tree, under which he was wont to rest on sultry days. One very warm afternoon he was sitting under this tree with two of his friends, fellow-gōshi, chatting and drinking wine, when he felt all of a sudden very drowsy—so drowsy that he begged his friends to excuse him for taking a nap in their presence. Then he lay down at the foot of the tree, and dreamed this dream:

He thought that as he was lying there in his garden, he saw a procession, like the train of some great daimyō, descending a hill near by, and that he got up to look at it. A very grand procession it proved to be—more imposing than anything of the kind which he had ever seen before; and it was advancing toward his dwelling. He observed in the van of it a number of young men richly appareled, who were drawing a great lacquered palace-carriage, or *gosho-guruma,* hung with bright blue silk. When the procession arrived within a short distance of the house it halted; and a richly dressed man—evidently a person of rank—advanced from it, approached Akinosuké, bowed to him profoundly, and then said:

"Honored Sir, you see before you a *kérai* [vassal] of the

Kokuō of Tokoyo.[1] My master, the King, commands me to greet you in his august name, and to place myself wholly at your disposal. He also bids me inform you that he augustly desires your presence at the palace. Be therefore pleased immediately to enter this honorable carriage, which he has sent for your conveyance."

Upon hearing these words Akinosuké wanted to make some fitting reply; but he was too much astonished and embarrassed for speech;—and in the same moment his will seemed to melt away from him, so that he could only do as the *kérai* bade him. He entered the carriage; the *kérai* took a place beside him, and made a signal; the drawers, seizing the silken ropes, turned the great vehicle southward—and the journey began.

In a very short time, to Akinosuké's amazement, the carriage stopped in front of a huge two-storied gateway (*rōmon*), of Chinese style, which he had never before seen. Here the *kérai* dismounted, saying, "I go to announce the honorable arrival,"—and he disappeared. After some little waiting, Akinosuké saw two noble-looking men, wearing robes of purple silk and high caps of the form indicating lofty rank, come from the gateway. These, after having respectfully saluted him, helped him to descend from the carriage, and led him through the great gate and across a vast garden to the entrance of a palace whose front appeared to extend, west and east, to a distance of miles. Akinosuké was then shown into a reception-room of wonderful size and splendor. His guides conducted him to the place of honor, and respectfully seated themselves apart; while serving-maids, in costume of ceremony, brought refreshments. When Akinosuké had partaken of the refreshments, the two purple-robed attendants bowed low before him, and addressed him in the following words—each speaking alternately, according to the etiquette of courts:

"It is now our honorable duty to inform you . . . as to the

[1] This name "Tokoyo" is indefinite. According to circumstances it may signify any unknown country—or that undiscovered country from whose bourn no traveler returns—or that Fairyland of far-eastern fable, the Realm of Hōrai. The term "Kokuō" means the ruler of a country—therefore a king. The original phrase, *Tokoyo no Kokuō,* might be rendered here as "the Ruler of Hōrai", or "the King of Fairyland".

reason of your having been summoned hither. . . . Our master, the King, augustly desires that you become his son-in-law; . . . and it is his wish and command that you shall wed this very day . . . the August Princess, his maiden-daughter. . . . We shall soon conduct you to the presence-chamber . . . where His Augustness even now is waiting to receive you. . . . But it will be necessary that we first invest you . . . with the appropriate garments of ceremony."[1]

Having thus spoken, the attendants rose together, and proceeded to an alcove containing a great chest of gold lacquer. They opened the chest, and took from it various robes and girdles of rich material, and a *kamuri,* or regal headdress. With these they attired Akinosuké as befitted a princely bridegroom; and he was then conducted to the presence-room, where he saw the Kokuō of Tokoyo seated upon the *daiza,*[2] wearing the high black cap of state, and robed in robes of yellow silk. Before the *daiza,* to the left and right, a multitude of dignitaries sat in rank, motionless and splendid as images in a temple; and Akinosuké, advancing into their midst, saluted the king with the triple prostration of usage. The king greeted him with gracious words, and then said:

"You have already been informed as to the reason of your having been summoned to Our presence. We have decided that you shall become the adopted husband of Our only daughter—and the wedding ceremony shall now be performed."

As the king finished speaking, a sound of joyful music was heard; and a long train of beautiful court ladies advanced from behind a curtain, to conduct Akinosuké to the room in which his bride awaited him.

The room was immense; but it could scarcely contain the multitude of guests assembled to witness the wedding ceremony. All bowed down before Akinosuké as he took his place, facing the King's daughter, on the kneeling-cushion prepared for him. As a maiden of heaven the bride appeared to be; and her robes

[1]The last phrase, according to old custom, had to be uttered by both attendants at the same time. All these ceremonial observances can still be studied on the Japanese stage.

[2]This was the name given to the estrade, or dais, upon which a feudal prince or ruler sat in state. The term literally signifies "great seat".

were beautiful as a summer sky. And the marriage was performed amid great rejoicing.

Afterwards the pair were conducted to a suite of apartments that had been prepared for them in another portion of the palace; and there they received the congratulations of many noble persons, and wedding gifts beyond counting.

Some days later Akinosuké was again summoned to the throne-room. On this occasion he was received even more graciously than before; and the King said to him:

"In the southwestern part of Our dominion there is an island called Raishū. We have now appointed you Governor of that island. You will find the people loyal and docile; but their laws have not yet been brought into proper accord with the laws of Tokoyo; and their customs have not been properly regulated. We entrust you with the duty of improving their social condition as far as may be possible; and We desire that you shall rule them with kindness and wisdom. All preparations necessary for your journey to Raishū have already been made."

So Akinosuké and his bride departed from the palace of Tokoyo, accompanied to the shore by a great escort of nobles and officials; and they embarked upon a ship of state provided by the king. And with favoring winds they safely sailed to Raishū, and found the good people of that island assembled upon the beach to welcome them.

Akinosuké entered at once upon his new duties; and they did not prove to be hard. During the first three years of his governorship he was occupied chiefly with the framing and the enactment of laws; but he had wise counselors to help him, and he never found the work unpleasant. When it was all finished, he had no active duties to perform, beyond attending the rites and ceremonies ordained by ancient custom. The country was so healthy and so fertile that sickness and want were unknown; and the people were so good that no laws were ever broken. And Akinosuké dwelt and ruled in Raishū for twenty years more—making in all twenty-three years of sojourn, during which no shadow of sorrow traversed his life.

But in the twenty-fourth year of his governorship, a great misfortune came upon him; for his wife, who had borne him seven children—five boys and two girls—fell sick and died. She was buried, with high pomp, on the summit of a beautiful hill in the district of Hanryōkō; and a monument, exceedingly splendid, was placed above her grave. But Akinosuké felt such grief at her death that he no longer cared to live.

Now when the legal period of mourning was over, there came to Raishū, from the Tokoyo palace, a *shisha,* or royal messenger. The *shisha* delivered to Akinosuké a message of condolence, and then said to him:—

"These are the words which our august master, the King of Tokoyo, commands that I repeat to you: 'We will now send you back to your own people and country. As for the seven children, they are the grandsons and the granddaughters of the King, and shall be fitly cared for. Do not, therefore, allow your mind to be troubled concerning them.'"

On receiving this mandate, Akinosuké submissively prepared for his departure. When all his affairs had been settled, and the ceremony of bidding farewell to his counselors and trusted officials had been concluded, he was escorted with much honor to the port. There he embarked upon the ship sent for him; and the ship sailed out into the blue sea, under the blue sky; and the shape of the island of Raishū itself turned blue, and then turned gray, and then vanished forever. . . . And Akinosuké suddenly awoke—under the cedar-tree in his own garden!

For the moment he was stupefied and dazed. But he perceived his two friends still seated near him—drinking and chatting merrily. He stared at them in a bewildered way, and cried aloud: "How strange!"

"Akinosuké must have been dreaming," one of them exclaimed, with a laugh. "What did you see, Akinosuké, that was strange?"

Then Akinosuké told his dream—that dream of three-and-twenty years' sojourn in the realm of Tokoyo, in the island of Raishū—and they were astonished, because he had really slept for no more than a few minutes.

One gōshi said:

"Indeed, you saw strange things. We also saw something strange while you were napping. A little yellow butterfly was fluttering over your face for a moment or two; and we watched it. Then it alighted on the ground beside you, close to the tree; and almost as soon as it alighted there, a big, big ant came out of a hole, and seized it and pulled it down into the hole. Just before you woke up, we saw that very butterfly come out of the hole again, and flutter over your face as before. And then it suddenly disappeared: we do not know where it went."

"Perhaps it was Akinosuké's soul," the other gōshi said; "certainly I thought I saw it fly into his mouth. . . . But, even if that butterfly *was* Akinosuké's soul, the fact would not explain his dream."

"The ants might explain it," returned the first speaker. "Ants are queer beings—possibly goblins. . . . Anyhow, there is a big ant's nest under that cedar-tree." . . .

"Let us look!" cried Akinosuké, greatly moved by this suggestion. Ane he went for a spade.

The ground about and beneath the cedar-tree proved to have been excavated, in a most surprising way, by a prodigious colony of ants. The ants had furthermore built inside their excavations; and their tiny constructions of straw, clay, and stems bore an odd resemblance to miniature towns. In the middle of a structure considerably larger than the rest there was a marvelous swarming of small ants around the body of one very big ant, which had yellowish wings and a long black head.

"Why, there is the King of my dream!" cried Akinosuké; "and there is the palace of Tokoyo! . . . How extraordinary! . . . Raishū ought to lie somewhere southwest of it—to the left of that big root. . . . Yes!—here it is! . . . How very strange! Now I am sure that I can find the mountain of Hanryōkō, and the grave of the princess." . . .

In the wreck of the nest he searched and searched, and at last discovered a tiny mound, on the top of which was fixed a water-worn pebble, in shape resembling a Buddhist monument. Underneath it he found—embedded in clay—the dead body of a female ant.

RIKI-BAKA

Riki-Baka

Riki-Baka

His name was Riki, signifying Strength; but the people called him Riki-the-Simple, or Riki-the-Fool—"Riki-Baka"— because he had been born into perpetual childhood. For the same reason they were kind to him—even when he set a house on fire by putting a lighted match to a mosquito-curtain, and clapped his hands for joy to see the blaze. At sixteen years he was a tall, strong lad; but in mind he remained always at the happy age of two, and therefore continued to play with very small children. The bigger children of the neighborhood, from four to seven years old, did not care to play with him, because he could not learn their songs and games. His favorite toy was a broomstick, which he used as a hobby-horse; and for hours at a time he would ride on that broomstick, up and down the slope in front of my house, with amazing peals of laughter. But at last he became troublesome by reason of his noise; and I had to tell him that he must find another playground. He bowed submissively, and then went off—sorrowfully trailing his broomstick behind him. Gentle at all times, and perfectly harmless if allowed no chance to play with fire, he seldom gave anybody cause for complaint. His relation to the life of our street was scarcely more than that of a dog or a chicken; and when he finally disappeared, I did not miss him. Months and months passed by before anything happened to remind me of Riki.

"What has become of Riki?" I then asked the old woodcutter who supplies our neighborhood with fuel. I remembered that Riki had often helped him to carry his bundles.

"Riki-Baka?" answered the old man. "Ah, Riki is dead—poor fellow! . . . Yes, he died nearly a year ago, very suddenly;

the doctors said that he had some disease of the brain. And there is a strange story now about that poor Riki.

"When Riki died, his mother wrote his name, 'Riki-Baka', in the palm of his left hand—putting 'Riki' in the Chinese character, and 'Baka' in *kana*. And she repeated many prayers for him—prayers that he might be reborn into some more happy condition.

"Now, about three months ago, in the honorable residence of Nanigashi-Sama, in Kōjimachi, a boy was born with characters on the palm of his left hand; and the characters were quite plain to read—'RIKI-BAKA'!

"So the people of that house knew that the birth must have happened in answer to somebody's prayer; and they caused inquiry to be made everywhere. At last a vegetable-seller brought word to them that there used to be a simple lad, called Riki-Baka, living in the Ushigomé quarter, and that he had died during the last autumn; and they sent two men-servants to look for the mother of Riki.

"Those servants found the mother of Riki, and told her what had happened; and she was glad exceedingly—for that Nanigashi house is a very rich and famous house. But the servants said that the family of Nanigashi-Sama were very angry about the word 'Baka' on the child's hand. 'And where is your Riki buried?' the servants asked. 'He is buried in the cemetery of Zendōji,' she told them. 'Please to give us some of the clay of his grave,' they requested.

"So she went with them to the temple Zendōji, and showed them Riki's grave; and they took some of the grave-clay away with them, wrapped up in a *furoshiki*.[1] . . . They gave Riki's mother some money—ten yen." . . .

"But what did they want with that clay?" I inquired.

"Well," the old man answered, "you know that it would not do to let the child grow up with that name on his hand. And there is no other means of removing characters that come in that way upon the body of a child: *you must rub the skin with clay taken from the grave of the body of the former birth*." . . .

[1] A square piece of cotton-goods, or other woven material, used as a wrapper in which to carry small packages.

HI-MAWARI

Hi-Mawari

Hi-Mawari

On the wooded hill behind the house Robert and I are looking for fairy-rings. Robert is eight years old, comely, and very wise; I am a little more than seven—and I reverence Robert. It is a glowing, glorious August day; and the warm air is filled with sharp, sweet scents of resin.

We do not find any fairy-rings; but we find a great many pine-cones in the high grass. . . . I tell Robert the old Welsh story of the man who went to sleep, unawares, inside of a fairy-ring, and so disappeared for seven years, and would never eat or speak after his friends had delivered him from the enchantment.

"They eat nothing but the points of needles, you know," says Robert.

"Who?" I ask.

"Goblins," Robert answers.

This revelation leaves me dumb with astonishment and awe. . . . But Robert suddenly cries out:

"There is a harper!—he is coming to the house!"

And down the hill we run to hear the harper. . . . But what a harper! Not like the hoary minstrels of the picture-books. A swarthy, sturdy, unkempt vagabond, with black bold eyes under scowling black brows. More like a bricklayer than a bard—and his garments are corduroy!

"Wonder if he is going to sing in Welsh?" murmurs Robert.

I feel too much disappointed to make any remarks. The

harper poses his harp—a huge instrument—upon our doorstep, sets all the strings ringing with a sweep of his grimy fingers, clears his throat with a sort of angry growl, and begins:

Believe me, if all those endearing young charms,
Which I gaze on so fondly to-day . . .

The accent, the attitude, the voice, all fill me with repulsion unutterable—shock me with a new sensation of formidable vulgarity. I want to cry out loud, "You have no right to sing that song!" For I have heard it sung by the lips of the dearest and fairest being in my little world; and that this rude, coarse man should dare to sing it vexes me like a mockery—angers me like an insolence. But only for a moment! . . . With the utterance of the syllables "to-day", that deep, grim voice suddently breaks into a quivering tenderness indescribable; then, marvelously changing, it mellows into tones sonorous and rich as the bass of a great organ, while a sensation unlike anything ever felt before takes me by the throat. . . . What witchcraft has he learned? what secret has he found—this scowling man of the road? . . . Oh! is there anybody else in the whole world who can sing like that? . . . And the form of the singer flickers and dims; —and the house, and the lawn, and all visible shapes of things tremble and swim before me. Yet instinctively I fear that man—I almost hate him; and I feel myself flushing with anger and shame because of his power to move me thus. . . .

"He made you cry," Robert compassionately observes, to my further confusion,—as the harper strides away, richer by a gift of sixpence taken without thanks. . . . "But I think he must be a gipsy. Gipsies are bad people—and they are wizards. . . . Let us go back to the wood."

We climb again to the pines, and there squat down upon the sun-flecked grass, and look over town and sea. But we do not play as before: the spell of the wizard is strong upon us both. . . . "Perhaps he is a goblin," I venture at last, "or a fairy?" "No," says Robert—"only a gipsy. But that is nearly as bad. They steal children, you know." . . .

"What shall we do if he comes up here?" I gasp, in sudden terror at the lonesomeness of our situation.

"Oh, he would n't dare," answers Robert—"not by daylight, you know."

*　　*
*

[Only yesterday, near the village of Takata, I noticed a flower which the Japanese call by nearly the same name as we do: *Himawari,* "The Sunward-turning"; and over the space of forty years there thrilled back to me the voice of that wandering harper:

As the Sunflower turns on her god, when he sets,
The same look that she turned when he rose.

Again I saw the sun-flecked shadows on that far Welsh hill; and Robert for a moment again stood beside me, with his girl's face and his curls of gold. We were looking for fairy-rings. . . . But all that existed of the real Robert must long ago have suffered a sea-change into something rich and strange. . . . *Greater love hath no man than this, that a man lay down his life for his friend. . . .*]

Hōrai

Hōrai

Blue vision of depth lost in height—sea and sky interblending through luminous haze. The day is of spring, and the hour morning.

Only sky and sea—one azure enormity. . . . In the fore, ripples are catching a silvery light, and threads of foam are swirling. But a little farther off no motion is visible, nor anything save color: dim warm blue of water widening away to melt into blue of air. Horizon there is none: only distance soaring into space—infinite concavity hollowing before you, and hugely arching above you—the color deepening with the height. But far in the midway-blue there hangs a faint, faint vision of palace towers, with high roofs horned and curved like moons—some shadowing of splendor strange and old, illumined by a sunshine soft as memory.

. . . What I have thus been trying to describe is a kakémono—that is to say, a Japanese painting on silk, suspended to the wall of my alcove; and the name of it is SHINKIRO, which signifies "Mirage". But the shapes of the mirage are unmistakable. Those are the glimmering portals of Hōrai the blest; and those are the moony roofs of the Palace of the Dragon-King; and the fashion of them (though limned by a Japanese brush of to-day) is the fashion of things Chinese, twenty-one hundred years ago. . . .

Thus much is told of the place in the Chinese books of that time:

In Hōrai there is neither death nor pain; and there is no winter. The flowers in that place never fade, and the fruits never fail; and if a man taste of those fruits even but once, he can never again feel thirst or hunger. In Hōrai grow the enchanted plants *So-rin-shi,* and *Riku-gō-aoi,* and *Ban-kon-tō,* which heal all manner of sickness; and there grows also the magical grass *Yō-shin-shi,* that quickens the dead; and the magical grass is watered by a fairy water of which a single drink confers perpetual youth. The people of Hōrai eat their rice out of very, very small bowls; but the rice never diminishes within those bowls—however much of it be eaten—until the eater desires no more. And the people of Hōrai drink their wine out of very, very small cups; but no man can empty one of those cups—however stoutly he may drink—until there comes upon him the pleasant drowsiness of intoxication.

All this and more is told in the legends of the time of the Shin dynasty. But that the people who wrote down those legends ever saw Hōrai, even in a mirage, is not believable. For really there are no enchanged fruits which leave the eater forever satisfied—nor any magical grass which revives the dead—nor any fountain of fairy water—nor any bowls which never lack rice—nor any cups which never lack wine. It is not true that sorrow and death never enter Hōrai; neither is it true that there is not any winter. The winter in Hōrai is cold; and winds then bite to the bone; and the heaping of snow is monstrous on the roofs of the Dragon-King.

Nevertheless there are wonderful things in Hōrai; and the most wonderful of all has not been mentioned by any Chinese writer. I mean the atmosphere of Hōrai. It is an atmosphere peculiar to the place; and, because of it, the sunshine in Hōrai is *whiter* than any other sunshine—a milky light that never dazzles—astonishingly clear, but very soft. This atmosphere is not of our human period: it is enormously old, so old that I feel afraid when I try to think how old it is; and it is not a mixture of nitrogen and oxygen. It is not made of air at all, but of ghost—the substance of quintillions of quintillions of generations of souls blended into one immense translucency—souls of people who thought in ways never resembling our ways. Whatever mortal man inhales that atmosphere, he takes into his blood the thrilling of these spirits; and they change the senses within him

—reshaping his notions of Space and Time—so that he can see only as they used to see, and feel only as they used to feel, and think only as they used to think. Soft as sleep are these changes of sense; and Hōrai, discerned across them, might thus be described:

—Because in Hōrai there is no knowledge of great evil, the hearts of the people never grow old. And, by reason of being always young in heart, the people of Hōrai smile from birth until death—except when the gods send sorrow among them; and faces then are veiled until the sorrow goes away. All folk in Hōrai love and trust each other, as if all were members of a single household; and the speech of the women is like birdsong, because the hearts of them are light as the souls of birds; and the swaying of the sleeves of the maidens at play seems a flutter of wide, soft wings. In Hōrai nothing is hidden but grief, because there is no reason for shame; and nothing is locked away, because there could not be any theft; and by night as well as by day all doors remain unbarred, because there is no reason for fear. And because the people are fairies—though mortal—all things in Hōrai, except the Palace of the Dragon-King, are small and quaint and queer; and these fairy-folk do really eat their rice out of very small bowls, and drink their wine out of very, very small cups. . . .

—Much of this seeming would be due to the inhalation of that ghostly atmosphere—but not all. For the spell wrought by the dead is only the charm of an Ideal, the glamour of an ancient hope; and something of that hope has found fulfillment in many hearts—in the simple beauty of unselfish lives—in the sweetness of Woman. . . .

—Evil winds from the West are blowing over Hōrai; and the magical atmosphere, alas! is shrinking away before them. It lingers now in patches only, and bands—like those long bright bands of cloud that trail across the landscapes of Japanese painters. Under these shreds of the elfish vapor you still can find Hōrai—but not elsewhere. . . . Remember that Hōrai is also called Shinkirō, which signifies Mirage—the Vision of the Intangible. And the Vision is fading—never again to appear save in pictures and poems and dreams. . . .

Insect Studies

BUTTERFLIES

Butterflies

Butterflies

I

Would that I could hope for the luck of that Chinese scholar known to Japanese literature as "Rōsan"! For he was beloved by two spirit-maidens, celestial sisters, who every ten days came to visit him and to tell him stories about butterflies. Now there are marvelous Chinese stories about butterflies—ghostly stories; and I want to know them. But never shall I be able to read Chinese, nor even Japanese; and the little Japanese poetry that I manage, with exceeding difficulty, to translate, contains so many allusions to Chinese stories of butterflies that I am tormented with the torment of Tantalus. . . . And, of course, no spirit-maidens will ever deign to visit so skeptical a person as myself.

I want to know, for example, the whole story of that Chinese maiden whom the butterflies took to be a flower, and followed in multitude—so fragrant and so fair was she. Also I should like to know something more concerning the butterflies of the Emperor Gensō, or Ming Hwang, who made them choose his loves for him. . . . He used to hold wine-parties in his amazing garden; and ladies of exceeding beauty were in attendance; and caged butterflies, set free among them, would fly to the fairest; and then, upon that fairest the Imperial favor was bestowed. But after Gensō Kōtei had seen Yōkihi (whom the Chinese call Yang-Kwei-Fei), he would not suffer the butterflies to choose for him—which was unlucky, as Yōkihi got him into serious trouble. . . . Again, I should like to know more about the experience of that Chinese scholar, celebrated in Japan under the name of

Sōshū, who dreamed that he was a butterfly, and had all the sensations of a butterfly in that dream. For his spirit had really been wandering about in the shape of a butterfly; and, when he awoke, the memories and the feelings of butterfly existence remained so vivid in his mind that he could not act like a human being. . . . Finally I should like to know the text of a certain Chinese official recognition of sundry butterflies as the spirits of an Emperor and of his attendants. . . .

Most of the Japanese literature about butterflies, excepting poetry, appears to be of Chinese origin; and even that old national æsthetic feeling on the subject, which found such delightful expression in Japanese art and song and custom, may have been first developed under Chinese teaching. Chinese precedent doubtless explains why Japanese poets and painters chose so often for their *geimyō*, or professional appellations, such names as *Chōmu* ("Butterfly-Dream"), *Ichō* ("Solitary Butterfly"), etc. And even to this day such *geimyō* as *Chōhana* ("Butterfly-Blossom"), *Chōkichi* ("Butterfly-Luck"), or *Chōnosuké* ("Butterfly-Help"), are affected by dancing-girls. Besides artistic names having reference to butterflies, there are still in use real personal names (*yobina*) of this kind—such as Kochō, or Chō, meaning "Butterfly". They are borne by women only, as a rule—though there are some strange exceptions. . . . And here I may mention that, in the province of Mutsu, there still exists the curious old custom of calling the youngest daughter in a family *Tekona*—which quaint word, obsolete elsewhere, signifies in Mutsu dialect a butterfly. In classic time this word signified also a beautiful woman. . . .

It is possible also that some weird Japanese beliefs about butterflies are of Chinese derivation; but these beliefs might be older than China herself. The most interesting one, I think, is that the soul of a *living* person may wander about in the form of a butterfly. Some pretty fancies have been evolved out of this belief—such as the notion that if a butterfly enters your guest-room and perches behind the bamboo screen, the person whom you most love is coming to see you. That a butterfly may be the spirit of somebody is not a reason for being afraid of it. Nevertheless there are times when even butterflies can inspire fear by appearing in prodigious numbers; and Japanese history records such an event. When Taïra-no-Masakado was secretly preparing for his famous revolt, there appeared in Kyōto so vast a swarm of butterflies that the people were frightened—thinking the apparition to be a portent of coming evil. . . . Perhaps those butterflies were supposed to be the spirits of the thousands doomed to perish in battle, and agitated on the eve of war by some mysterious premonition of death.

However, in Japanese belief, a butterfly may be the soul of a dead person as well as of a living person. Indeed it is a custom of souls to take butterfly-shape in order to announce the fact of their final departure from the body; and for this reason any butterfly which enters a house ought to be kindly treated.

To this belief, and to queer fancies connected with it, there are many allusions in popular drama. For example, there is a well-known play called *Tondé-déru-Kochō-no-Kanzashi;* or, "The Flying Hairpin of Kochō". Kochō is a beautiful person who kills herself because of false accusations and cruel treatment. Her would-be avenger long seeks in vain for the author of the wrong. But at last the dead woman's hairpin turns into a butterfly, and serves as a guide to vengeance by hovering above the place where the villain is hiding.

—Of course those big paper butterflies (*o-chō* and *mé-chō*) which figure at weddings must not be thought of as having any ghostly signification. As emblems they only express the joy of loving union, and the hope that the newly married couple may pass through life together as a pair of butterflies flit lightly through some pleasant garden—now hovering upward, now downward, but never widely separating.

II

A small selection of *hokku* on butterflies will help to illustrate Japanese interest in the æsthetic side of the subject. Some are pictures only—tiny color-sketches made with seventeen syllables;

some are nothing more than pretty fancies, or graceful suggestions; but the reader will find variety. Probably he will not care much for the verses in themselves. The taste for Japanese poetry of the epigrammatic sort is a taste that must be slowly acquired; and it is only by degrees, after patient study, that the possibilities of such composition can be fairly estimated. Hasty criticism has declared that to put forward any serious claim on behalf of seventeen-syllable poems "would be absurd". But what, then, of Crashaw's famous line upon the miracle at the marriage feast in Cana?—

Nympha pudica Deum vidit, et erubuit.[1]

Only fourteen syllables—and immortality. Now with seventeen Japanese syllables things quite as wonderful—indeed, much more wonderful—have been done, not once or twice, but probably a thousand times. . . . However, there is nothing wonderful in the following *hokku,* which have been selected for more than literary reasons:

Nugi-kakuru[2]
Haori sugata no
Kochō kana!

[*Like a* haori *being taken off—that is the shape of a butterfly!*]

[1]"The modest nymph beheld her God, and blushed." (Or, in a more familiar rendering: "The modest water saw its God, and blushed.") In this line the double value of the word *nympha*—used by classical poets both in the meaning of fountain and in that of the divinity of a fountain, or spring—reminds one of that graceful playing with words which Japanese poets practice.

[2]More usually written *nugi-kakéru,* which means either "to take off and hang up", or "to begin to take off", as in the above poem. More loosely, but more effectively, the verses might thus be rendered: "Like a woman slipping off her haori—that is the appearance of a butterfly." One must have seen the Japanese garment described, to appreciate the comparison. The haori is a silk upper-dress—a kind of sleeved cloak—worn by both sexes; but the poem suggests a woman's *haori,* which is usually of richer color or material. The sleeves are wide; and the lining is usually of brightly colored silk, often beautifully variegated. In taking off the haori, the brilliant lining is displayed, and at such an instant the fluttering splendor might well be likened to the appearance of a butterfly in motion.

Torisashi no
Sao no jama suru,
Kochō kana!

[*Ah, the butterfly keeps getting in the way of the bird-catcher's pole!*[1]]

Tsurigané ni
Tomarité nemuru
Kochō kana!

[*Perched upon the temple-bell, the butterfly sleeps!*]

Néru-uchi mo
Asobu-yumé wo ya—
Kusa no chō!

[*Even while sleeping, its dream is of play—ah, the butterfly of the grass!*[2]]

Oki, oki yo!
Waga tomo ni sen,
Néru-kochō!

[*Wake up! wake up!—I will make thee my comrade, thou sleeping butterfly.*[3]]

Kago no tori
Chō wo urayamu
Metsuki kana!

[*Ah, the sad expression in the eyes of that caged bird!—envying the butterfly!*]

Chō tondé—
Kazé naki hi to mo
Miëzari ki!

[1] The bird-catcher's pole is smeared with bird-lime; and the verses suggest that the insect is preventing the man from using his pole by persistently getting in the way of it—as the birds might take warning from seeing the butterfly limed. *Jama suru* means "to hinder" or "prevent".

[2] Even while it is resting, the wings of the butterfly may be seen to quiver at moments—as if the creature were dreaming of flight.

[3] A little poem by Bashō, greatest of all Japanese composers of *hokku*. The verses are intended to suggest the joyous feeling of spring-time.

[*Even though it did not appear to be a windy day,*[1] *the fluttering of the butterflies——!*]

Rakkwa éda ni
Kaëru to miréba—
Kochō kana!

[*When I saw the fallen flower return to the branch—lo! it was only a butterfly!*[2]]

Chiru-hana ni—
Karusa arasoü
Kochō kana!

[*How the butterfly strives to compete in lightness with the falling flowers!*[3]]

Chōchō ya!
Onna no michi no
Ato ya saki!

[*See that butterfly on the woman's path—now fluttering behind her, now before!*]

Chōchō ya!
Hana-nusubito wo
Tsukété-yuku!

[*Ha! the butterfly!—it is following the person who stole the flowers!*]

Aki no chō
Tomo nakéréba ya;
Hito ni tsuku.

[1] Literally, "a windless day"; but two negatives in Japanese poetry do not necessarily imply an affirmative, as in English. The meaning is, that although there is no wind, the fluttering motion of the butterflies suggests, to the eyes at least, that a strong breeze is playing.

[2] Alluding to the Buddhist proverb: *Rakkwa éda ni kaërazu; ha-kyō futatabi terasazu* ("The fallen flower returns not to the branch; the broken mirror never again reflects."). So says the proverb—yet is seemed to me that I saw a fallen flower return to the branch. . . . No: it was only a butterfly.

[3] Alluding probably to the light fluttering motion of falling cherry-petals.

[*Poor autumn butterfly!—when left without a comrade* (of its own race), *it follows after man* (or "a person")!]

Owarété mo,
Isoganu furi no
Chōcho kana!

[*Ah, the butterfly! Even when chased, it never has the air of being in a hurry.*]

Chō wa mina
Jiu-shichi-hachi no
Sugata kana!

[*As for butterflies, they all have the appearance of being the about seventeen or eighteen years old.*[1]]

Chō tobu ya—
Kono yo no urami
Naki yō ni!

[*How the butterfly sports—just as if there were no enmity* (or "envy") *in this world!*]

Chō tobu ya,
Kono yo ni nozomi
Nai yō ni!

[*Ah, the butterfly!—it sports about as if it had nothing more to desire in this present state of existence.*]

Nami no hana ni
Tomari kanétaru,
Kochō kana!

[*Having found it difficult indeed to perch upon the* (*foam-*) *blossoms of the waves—alas for the butterfly!*]

[1] That is to say, the grace of their motion makes one think of the grace of young girls, daintily costumed, in robes with long fluttering sleeves. . . . An old Japanese proverb declares that even a devil is pretty at eighteen: *Oni mo jiuhachi azami no hana:* "Even a devil at eighteen, flower-of-the-thistle."

Mutsumashi ya!—
Umaré-kawaraba
Nobé no chō.[1]

[*If (in our next existence) we be born into the state of butterflies upon the moor, then perchance we may be happy together!*]

Nadéshiko ni
Chōchō shiroshi—
Taré no kon?[2]

[*On the pink-flower there is a white butterfly: whose spirit, I wonder?*]

Ichi-nichi no
Tsuma to miëkéri—
Chō futatsu.

[*The one-day wife has at last appeared—a pair of butterflies!*]

Kité wa maü,
Futari shidzuka no
Kochō kana!

[*Approaching they dance; but when the two meet at last they are very quiet, the butterflies!*]

Chō wo oü
Kokoro-mochitashi
Itsumadémo!

[*Would that I might always have the heart* (desire) *of chasing butterflies!*[3]]

*

* *

Besides these specimens of poetry about butterflies, I have

[1] Or perhaps the verses might be more effectively rendered thus: "Happy together, do you say? Yes—if we should be reborn as field-butterflies in some future life: then we might accord!" This poem was composed by the celebrated poet Issa, on the occasion of divorcing his wife.

[2] Or, *Taré no tama?*

[3] Literally, "Butterfly-pursuing heart I wish to have always";—*i.e.,* I would that I might always be able to find pleasure in simple things like a happy child.

one queer example to offer of Japanese prose literature on the same topic. The original, of which I have attempted only a free translation, can be found in the curious old book *Mushi-Isamé* ("Insect-Admonitions"); and it assumes the form of a discourse to a butterfly. But it is really a didactic allegory—suggesting the moral significance of a social rise and fall:

"Now, under the sun of spring, the winds are gentle, and flowers pinkly bloom, and grasses are soft, and the hearts of people are glad. Butterflies everywhere flutter joyously: so many persons now compose Chinese verses and Japanese verses about butterflies.

"And this season, O Butterfly, is indeed the season of your bright prosperity: so comely you now are that in the whole world there is nothing more comely. For that reason all other insects admire and envy you—there is not among them even one that does not envy you. Nor do insects alone regard you with envy: men also both envy and admire you. Sōshū of China, in a dream, assumed your shape; Sakoku of Japan, after dying, took your form, and therein made ghostly apparition. Nor is the envy that you inspire shared only by insects and mankind: even things without soul change their form into yours: witness the barley-grass, which turns into a butterfly.[1]

"And therefore you are lifted up with pride, and think to yourself: 'In all this world there is nothing superior to me!' Ah! I can very well guess what is in your heart: you are too much satisfied with your own person. That is why you let yourself be blown thus lightly about by every wind; that is why you never remain still—always, always thinking: 'In the whole world there is no one so fortunate as I'.

"But now try to think a little about your own personal history. It is worth recalling; for there is a vulgar side to it. How a vulgar side? Well, for a considerable time after you were born, you had no such reason for rejoicing in your form. You were then a mere cabbage-insect, a hairy worm; and you were so poor that you could not afford even one robe to cover your nakedness;

[1] An old popular error—probably imported from China.

and your appearance was altogether disgusting. Everybody in those days hated the sight of you. Indeed you had good reason to be ashamed of yourself; and so ashamed you were that you collected old twigs and rubbish to hide in, and you made a hiding-nest, and hung it to a branch—and then everybody cried out at you, 'Raincoat Insect!' (*Mino-mushi*).[1] And during that period of your life, your sins were grievous. Among the tender green leaves of beautiful cherry-trees you and your fellows assembled, and there made ugliness extraordinary; and the expectant eyes of the people, who came from far away to admire the beauty of those cherry-trees, were hurt by the sight of you. And of things even more hateful than this you were guilty. You knew that poor, poor men and women had been cultivating *daikon* in their fields,—toiling and toiling under the hot sun till their hearts were filled with bitterness by reason of having to care for that *daikon;* and you persuaded your companions to go with you, and to gather upon the leaves of that *daikon,* and on the leaves of other vegetables planted by those poor people. Out of your greediness you ravaged those leaves, and gnawed them into all shapes of ugliness—caring nothing for the trouble of those poor folk. . . . Yes, such a creature you were, and such were your doings.

"And now that you have a comely form, you despise your old comrades, the insects; and, whenever you happen to meet any of them, you pretend not to know them [literally, 'You make an I-don't-know face']. Now you want to have none but wealthy and exalted people for friends. . . . Ah! you have forgotten the old times, have you?

"It is true that many people have forgotten your past, and are charmed by the sight of your present graceful shape and white wings, and write Chinese verses and Japanese verses about you. The high-born damsel, who could not bear even to look at you in your former shape, now gazes at you with delight, and wants you to perch upon her hairpin, and holds out her dainty

[1] A name suggested by the resemblance of the larva's artificial covering to the *mino,* or straw-raincoat, worn by Japanese peasants. I am not sure whether the dictionary rendering, "basket-worm", is quite correct; but the larva commonly called *minomushi* does really construct for itself something much like the covering of the basket-worm.

fan in the hope that you will light upon it. But this reminds me that there is an ancient Chinese story about you, which is not pretty.

"In the time of the Emperor Gensō, the Imperial Palace contained hundreds and thousands of beautiful ladies—so many, indeed, that it would have been difficult for any man to decide which among them was the loveliest. So all of those beautiful persons were assembled together in one place; and you were set free to fly among them; and it was decreed that the damsel upon whose hairpin you perched should be augustly summoned to the Imperial Chamber. In that time there could not be more than one Empress—which was a good law; but, because of you, the Emperor Gensō did great mischief in the land. For your mind is light and frivolous; and although among so many beautiful women there must have been some persons of pure heart, you would look for nothing but beauty, and so betook yourself to the person most beautiful in outward appearance. Therefore many of the female attendants ceased altogether to think about the right way of women, and began to study how to make themselves appear splendid in the eyes of men. And the end of it was that the Emperior Gensō died a pitiful and painful death—all because of your light and trifling mind. Indeed, your real character can easily be seen from your conduct in other matters. There are trees, for example—such as the evergreen-oak and the pine—whose leaves do not fade and fall, but remain always green; these are trees of firm heart, trees of solid character. But you say that they are stiff and formal; and you hate the sight of them, and never pay them a visit. Only to the cherry-tree, and the *kaido,*[1] and the peony, and the yellow rose you go: those you like because they have showy flowers, and you try only to please them. Such conduct, let me assure you, is very unbecoming. Those trees certainly have handsome flowers; but hunger-satisfying fruits they have not; and they are grateful to those only who are fond of luxury and show. And that is just the reason why they are pleased by your fluttering wings and delicate shape; that is why they are kind to you.

"Now, in this spring season, while you sportively dance

[1] *Pyrus spectabilis.*

through the gardens of the wealthy, or hover among the beautiful alleys of cherry-trees in blossom, you say to yourself: 'Nobody in the world has such pleasure as I, or such excellent friends. And, in spite of all that people may say, I most love the peony—and the golden yellow rose is my own darling, and I will obey her every least behest; for that is my pride and my delight'. . . . So you say. But the opulent and elegant season of flowers is very short: soon they will fade and fall. Then, in the time of summer heat, there will be green leaves only; and presently the winds of autumn will blow, when even the leaves themselves will shower down like rain, *parari-parari.* And your fate will then be as the fate of the unlucky in the proverb, *Tanomi ki no shita ni amé furu* [Even through the tree on which I relied for shelter the rain leaks down]. For you will seek out your old friend, the root-cutting insect, the grub, and beg him to let you return into your old-time hole; but now having wings, you will not be able to enter the hole because of them, and you will not be able to shelter your body anywhere between heaven and earth, and all the moor-grass will then have withered, and you will not have even one drop of dew with which to moisten your tongue—and there will be nothing left for you to do but to lie down and die. All because of your light and frivolous heart—but, ah! how lamentable an end!" . . .

III

Most of the Japanese stories about butterflies appear, as I have said, to be of Chinese origin. But I have one which is probably indigenous; and it seems to me worth telling for the benefit of persons who believe that there is no "romantic love" in the Far East.

Behind the cemetery of the temple of Sōzanji, in the suburbs of the capital, there long stood a solitary cottage, occupied by an old man named Takahama. He was liked in the neighborhood, by reason of his amiable ways; but almost everybody supposed him to be a little mad. Unless a man take the Buddhist vows, he is expected to marry, and to bring up a family. But

Takahama did not belong to the religious life; and he could not be persuaded to marry. Neither had he ever been known to enter into a love-relation with any woman. For more than fifty years he had lived entirely alone.

One summer he fell sick, and knew that he had not long to live. He then sent for his sister-in-law, a widow, and for her only son,—a lad of about twenty years old, to whom he was much attached. Both promptly came, and did whatever they could to soothe the old man's last hours.

One sultry afternoon, while the widow and her son were watching at his bedside, Takahama fell asleep. At the same moment a very large white butterfly entered the room, and perched upon the sick man's pillow. The nephew drove it away with a fan; but it returned immediately to the pillow, and was again driven away, only to come back a third time. Then the nephew chased it into the garden, and across the garden, through an open gate, into the cemetery of the neighboring temple. But it continued to flutter before him as if unwilling to be driven further, and acted so queerly that he began to wonder whether it was really a butterfly, or a *ma*.[1] He again chased it, and followed it far into the cemetery, until he saw it fly against a tomb—a woman's tomb. There it unaccountably disappeared; and he searched for it in vain. He then examined the monument. It bore the personal name "Akiko", together with an unfamiliar family name, and an inscription stating that Akiko had died at the age of eighteen. Apparently the tomb had been erected about fifty years previously; moss had begun to gather upon it. But it had been well cared for: there were fresh flowers before it; and the water-tank had recently been filled.

On returning to the sick room, the young man was shocked by the announcement that his uncle had ceased to breathe. Death had come to the sleeper painlessly; and the dead face smiled.

The young man told his mother of what he had seen in the cemetery.

"Ah!" exclaimed the widow, "then it must have been Akiko!"...

[1] An evil spirit.

"But who was Akiko, mother?" the nephew asked.

The widow answered:

"When your good uncle was young he was betrothed to a charming girl called Akiko, the daughter of a neighbor. Akiko died of consumption, only a little before the day appointed for the wedding; and her promised husband sorrowed greatly. After Akiko had been buried, he made a vow never to marry; and he built this little house beside the cemetery, so that he might be always near her grave. All this happened more than fifty years ago. And every day of those fifty years—winter and summer alike—your uncle went to the cemetery, and prayed at the grave, and swept the tomb, and set offerings before it. But he did not like to have any mention made of the matter; and he never spoke of it. . . . So, at last, Akiko came for him: the white butterfly was her soul."

IV

I had almost forgotten to mention an ancient Japanese dance, called the Butterfly Dance (*Kochō-Mai*), which used to be performed in the Imperial Palace, by dancers costumed as butterflies. Whether it is danced occasionally nowadays I do not know. It is said to be very difficult to learn. Six dancers are required for the proper performance of it; and they must move in particular figures—obeying traditional rules for every step, pose or gesture—and circling about each other very slowly to the sound of hand-drums and great drums, small flutes and great flutes, and pandean pipes of a form unknown to Western Pan.

MOSQUITOES

Mosquitoes

Mosquitoes

With a view to self-protection I have been reading Dr. Howard's book, "Mosquitoes". I am persecuted by mosquitoes. There are several species in my neighborhood; but only one of them is a serious torment—a tiny needly thing, all silver-speckled and silver-streaked. The puncture of it is sharp as an electric burn; and the mere hum of it has a lancinating quality of tone which foretells the quality of the pain about to come—much in the same way that a particular smell suggests a particular taste. I find that this mosquito much resembles the creature which Dr. Howard calls *Stegomyia fasciata,* or *Culex fasciatus:* and that its habits are the same as those of the *Stegomyia.* For example, it is diurnal rather than nocturnal, and becomes most troublesome during the afternoon. And I have discovered that it comes from the Buddhist cemetery—a very old cemetery—in the rear of my garden.

Dr. Howard's book declares that, in order to rid a neighborhood of mosquitoes, it is only necessary to pour a little petroleum, or kerosene oil, into the stagnant water where they breed. Once a week the oil should be used, "at the rate of one ounce for every fifteen square feet of water-surface, and a proportionate quantity for any less surface" . . . . But please to consider the conditions in *my* neighborhood!

I have said that my tormentors come from the Buddhist cemetery. Before nearly every tomb in that old cemetery there is a water-receptacle, or cistern, called *mizutamé*. In the majority of cases this *mizutamé* is simply an oblong cavity chiseled in the broad pedestal supporting the monument; but before tombs of a costly kind, having no pedestal-tank, a larger separate tank is placed, cut out of a single block of stone, and decorated with a family crest, or with symbolic carvings. In front of a tomb of the humblest class, having no *mizutamé,* water is placed in cups or other vessels—for the dead must have water. Flowers also must be offered to them; and before every tomb you will find a pair of bamboo cups, or other flower-vessels; and these, of course, contain water. There is a well in the cemetery to supply water for the graves. Whenever the tombs are visited by relatives and friends of the dead, fresh water is poured into the tanks and cups. But as an old cemetery of this kind contains thousands of *mizutamé,* and tens of thousands of flower-vessels, the water in all of these cannot be renewed every day. It becomes stagnant and populous. The deeper tanks seldom get dry—the rainfall at Tōkyō being heavy enough to keep them partly filled during nine months out of the twelve.

Well, it is in these tanks and flower-vessels that mine enemies are born: they rise by millions from the water of the dead—and, according to Buddhist doctrine, some of them may be reincarnations of those very dead, condemned by the error of former lives to the condition of *Jiki-ketsu-gaki,* or blood-drinking pretas. . . . Anyhow the malevolence of the *Culex fasciatus* would justify the suspicion that some wicked human soul had been compressed into that wailing speck of a body. . . .

Now, to return to the subject of kerosene-oil, you can exterminate the mosquitoes of any locality by covering with a film of kerosene all stagnant water surfaces therein. The larvae die on rising to breathe; and the adult females perish when they approach the water to launch their rafts of eggs. And I read, in Dr. Howard's book, that the actual cost of freeing from mosquitoes one American town of fifty thousand inhabitants, does not exceed three hundred dollars! . . .

I wonder what would be said if the city government of

Tōkyō—which is aggressively scientific and progressive—were suddenly to command that all water-surfaces in the Buddhist cemeteries should be covered, at regular intervals, with a film of kerosene oil! How could the religion which prohibits the taking of any life—even of invisible life—yield to such a mandate? Would filial piety even dream of consenting to obey such an order? And then to think of the cost, in labor and time, of putting kerosene oil, every seven days, into the millions of *mizu-tamé,* and the tens of millions of bamboo flower-cups, in the Tōkyō graveyards! . . . Impossible! To free the city from mosquitoes it would be necessary to demolish the ancient graveyards—and that would signify the ruin of the Buddhist temples attached to them—and that would mean the disparition of so many charming gardens, with their lotus-ponds and Sanscrit-lettered monuments and humpy bridges and holy groves and weirdly smiling Buddhas! So the extermination of the *Culex fasciatus* would involve the destruction of the poetry of the ancestral cult—surely too great a price to pay! . . .

Besides, I should like, when my time comes, to be laid away in some Buddhist graveyard of the ancient kind—so that my ghostly company should be ancient, caring nothing for the fashions and the changes and the disintegrations of Meiji. That old cemetery behind my garden would be a suitable place. Everything there is beautiful with a beauty of exceeding and startling queerness; each tree and stone has been shaped by some old, old ideal which no longer exists in any living brain; even the shadows are not of this time and sun, but of a world forgotten, that never knew steam or electricity or magnetism or—kerosene oil! Also in the boom of the big bell there is a quaintness of tone which wakens feelings, so strangely far-away from all the nineteen-century part of me, that the faint blind stirrings of them make me afraid,—deliciously afraid. Never do I hear that billowing peal but I become aware of a striving and a fluttering in the abyssal part of my ghost—a sensation as of memories struggling to reach the light beyond the obscurations of a million million deaths and births. I hope to remain within hearing of that bell. . . . And, considering the possibility of being doomed to the state of a *Jiki-ketsu-gaki,* I want to have my chance of being reborn in some bamboo flower-cup, or *mizutamé,* whence I might issue softly, singing my thin and pungent song, to bite some people that I know.

ANTS

Ants

Ants

I

This morning sky, after the night's tempest, is a pure and dazzling blue. The air—the delicious air!—is full of sweet resinous odors, shed from the countless pine-boughs broken and strewn by the gale. In the neighboring bamboo-grove I hear the flute-call of the bird that praises the Sūtra of the Lotos; and the land is very still by reason of the south wind. Now the summer, long delayed, is truly with us: butterflies of queer Japanese colors are flickering about; semi are wheezing; wasps are humming; gnats are dancing in the sun; and the ants are busy repairing their damaged habitations. . . . I bethink me of a Japanese poem:

Yuku é naki:
Ari no sumai ya!
Go-getsu amé.

[*Now the poor creature has nowhere to go! . . . Alas for the dwellings of the ants in this rain of the fifth month!*]

But those big black ants in my garden do not seem to need any sympathy. They have weathered the storm in some unimaginable way, while great trees were being uprooted, and houses blown to fragments, and roads washed out of existence. Yet, before the typhoon, they took no other visible precaution than to block up the gates of their subterranean town. And the spectacle of their triumphant toil to-day impels me to attempt an essay on Ants.

I should have liked to preface my disquisitions with something from the old Japanese literature—something emotional or metaphysical. But all that my Japanese friends were able to find for me on the subject—excepting some verses of little worth—was Chinese. This Chinese material consisted chiefly of strange stories; and one of them seems to me worth quoting—*faute de mieux.*

* *
*

In the province of Taishū, in China, there was a pious man who, every day, during many years, fervently worshipped a certain goddess. One morning, while he was engaged in his devotions, a beautiful woman, wearing a yellow robe, came into his chamber and stood before him. He, greatly surprised, asked her what she wanted, and why she had entered unannounced. She answered: "I am not a woman: I am the goddess whom you have so long and so faithfully worshipped; and I have now come to prove to you that your devotion has not been in vain. . . . Are you acquainted with the language of ants?" The worshipper replied: "I am only a low-born and ignorant person—not a scholar; and even of the language of superior men I know nothing." At these words the goddess smiled, and drew from her bosom a little box, shaped like an incense box. She opened the box, dipped a finger into it, and took therefrom some kind of ointment with which she anointed the ears of the man. "Now," she said to him, "try to find some ants, and when you find any, stoop down, and listen carefully to their talk. You will be able to understand it; and you will hear of something to your advantage. . . . Only remember that you must not frighten or vex the ants." Then the goddess vanished away.

The man immediately went out to look for some ants. He had scarcely crossed the threshold of his door when he perceived two ants upon a stone supporting one of the house-pillars. He stooped over them, and listened; and he was astonished to find that he could hear them talking, and could understand what they said. "Let us try to find a warmer place," proposed one of the ants. "Why a warmer place?" asked the other: "what is the matter with this place?" "It is too damp and cold below," said the first ant; "there is a big treasure buried here; and the sunshine cannot warm the ground about it." Then the two ants went away together, and the listener ran for a spade.

By digging in the neighborhood of the pillar, he soon found a number of large jars full of gold coin. The discovery of this treasure made him a very rich man.

Afterwards he often tried to listen to the conversation of ants. But he was never again able to hear them speak. The ointment of the goddess had opened his ears to their mysterious language for only a single day.

* *
*

Now I, like that Chinese devotee, must confess myself a very ignorant person, and naturally unable to hear the conversation of ants. But the Fairy of Science sometimes touches my ears and eyes with her wand; and then, for a little time, I am able to hear things inaudible, and to perceive things imperceptible.

II

For the same reason that it is considered wicked, in sundry circles, to speak of a non-Christian people having produced a civilization ethically superior to our own, certain persons will not be pleased by what I am going to say about ants. But there are men, incomparably wiser than I can ever hope to be, who think about insects and civilizations independently of the blessings of Christianity; and I find encouragement in the new *Cambridge Natural History,* which contains the following remarks by Professor David Sharp, concerning ants:

"Observation has revealed the most remarkable phenomena in the lives of these insects. Indeed we can scarcely avoid the conclusion that they have acquired, in many respects, the art of living together in societies more perfectly than our own species has; and that they have anticipated us in the acquisition of some of the industries and arts that greatly facilitate social life."

I suppose that few well-informed persons will dispute this

plain statement by a trained specialist. The contemporary man of science is not apt to become sentimental about ants or bees; but he will not hesitate to acknowledge that, in regard to social evolution, these insects appear to have advanced "beyond man". Herbert Spencer, whom nobody will charge with romantic tendencies, goes considerably further than Professor Sharp; showing us that ants are, in a very real sense, *ethically* as well as economically in advance of humanity—their lives being entirely devoted to altruistic ends. Indeed, Professor Sharp somewhat needlessly qualifies his praise of the ant with this cautious observation:

"The competence of the ant is not like that of man. It is devoted to the welfare of the species rather than to that of the individual, which is, as it were, sacrified or specialized for the benefit of the community."

The obvious implication—that any social state, in which the improvement of the individual is sacrificed to the common welfare, leaves much to be desired—is probably correct from the actual human standpoint. For man is yet imperfectly evolved; and human society has much to gain from his further individuation. But in regard to social insects the implied criticism is open to question. "The improvement of the individual," says Herbert Spencer, "consists in the better fitting of him for social coöperation; and this, being conducive to social prosperity, is conducive to the maintenance of the race." In other words, the value of the individual can be *only* in relation to the society; and this granted, whether the sacrifice of the individual for the sake of that society be good or evil must depend upon what the society might gain or lose through a further individuation of its members. . . . But, as we shall presently see, the conditions of ant-society that most deserve our attention are the ethical conditions; and these are beyond human criticism, since they realize that ideal of moral evolution described by Mr. Spencer as "a state in which egoism and altruism are so conciliated that the one merges into the other". That is to say, a state in which the only possible pleasure is the pleasure of unselfish action. Or, again to quote Mr.

Spencer, the activities of the insect-society are "activities which postpone individual well-being so completely to the well-being of the community that individual life appears to be attended to only just so far as is necessary to make possible due attention to social life, . . . the individual taking only just such food and just such rest as are needful to maintain its vigor".

III

I hope my reader is aware that ants practise horticulture and agriculture; that they are skillful in the cultivation of mushrooms; that they have domesticated (according to present knowledge) five hundred and eighty-four different kinds of animals; that they make tunnels through solid rock; that they know how to provide against atmospheric changes which might endanger the health of their children; and that, for insects, their longevity is exceptional—members of the more highly evolved species living for a considerable number of years.

But is is not especially of these matters that I wish to speak. What I want to talk about is the awful propriety, the terrible morality, of the ant.[1] Our most appalling ideals of conduct fall short of the ethics of the ant—as progress is reckoned in time—by nothing less then millions of years! . . When I say "the ant", I mean the highest type of ant—not, of course, the entire ant-family. About two thousand species of ants are already known; and these exhibit, in their social organizations, widely varying degrees of evolution. Certain social phenomena of the greatest biological importance, and of no less importance in their strange relation to the subject of ethics, can be studied to advantage only in the existence of the most highly evolved societies of ants.

After all that has been written of late years about the probable value of relative experience in the long life of the ant, I suppose that few persons would venture to deny individual

[1] An interesting fact in this connection is that the Japanese word for ant, *ari,* is represented by an ideograph formed of the character for "insect" combined with the character signifying "moral rectitude", "propriety" *(giri).* So the Chinese character actually means "The Propriety-Insect".

character to the ant. The intelligence of the little creature in meeting and overcoming difficulties of a totally new kind, and in adapting itself to conditions entirely foreign to its experience, proves a considerable power of independent thinking. But this at least is certain: that the ant has no individuality capable of being exercised in a purely selfish direction—I am using the word "selfish" in its ordinary acceptation. A greedy ant, a sensual ant, an ant capable of any one of the seven deadly sins, or even of a small venial sin, is unimaginable. Equally unimaginable, of course, a romantic ant, an ideological ant, a poetical ant, or an ant inclined to metaphysical speculations. No human mind could attain to the absolute matter-of-fact quality of the ant-mind; no human being, as now constituted, could cultivate a mental habit so impeccably practical as that of the ant. But this superlatively practical mind is incapable of moral error. It would be difficult, perhaps, to prove that the ant has no religious ideas. But it is certain that such ideas could not be of any use to it. The being incapable of moral weakness is beyond the need of "spiritual guidance".

Only in a vague way can we conceive the character of ant-society, and the nature of ant-morality; and to do even this we must try to imagine some yet impossible state of human society and human morals. Let us, then, imagine a world full of people incessantly and furiously working—all of whom seem to be women. No one of these women could be persuaded or deluded into taking a single atom of food more than is needful to maintain her strength; and no one of them ever sleeps a second longer than is necessary to keep her nervous system in good working order. And all of them are so peculiarly constituted that the least unnecessary indulgence would result in some derangement of function.

The work daily performed by these female laborers comprises road-making, bridge-building, timber-cutting, architectural construction of numberless kinds, horticulture and agriculture, the feeding and sheltering of a hundred varieties of domestic animals, the manufacture of sundry chemical products, the storage and conservation of countless foodstuffs, and the care of the children of the race. All this labor is done for the commonwealth — no citizen of which is capable even of thinking about "property", except as a *res publica;* and the sole object of the commonwealth is the nurture and training of its young, nearly all of whom are girls. The period of infancy is long; the children remain for a great while, not only helpless, but shapeless, and withal so delicate that they must be very carefully guarded against the least change of temperature. Fortunately their nurses understand the laws of health: each thoroughly knows all that she ought to know in regard to ventilation, disinfection, drainage, moisture, and the danger of germs — germs being as visible, perhaps, to her myopic sight as they become to our own eyes under the microscope. Indeed, all matters of hygiene are so well comprehended that no nurse ever makes a mistake about the sanitary conditions of her neighborhood.

In spite of this perpetual labor no worker remains unkempt: each is scrupulously neat, making her toilet many times a day. But as every worker is born with the most beautiful of combs and brushes attached to her wrists, no time is wasted in the toilet-room. Besides keeping themselves strictly clean, the workers must also keep their houses and gardens in faultless order, for the sake of the children. Nothing less than an earthquake, an eruption, an inundation, or a desperate war, is allowed to interrupt the daily routine of dusting, sweeping, scrubbing, and disinfecting.

IV

Now for stranger facts:

This world of incessant toil is a more than Vestal world. It is true that males can sometimes be perceived in it; but they appear only at particular seasons, and they have nothing whatever to do with the workers or with the work. None of them would presume to address a worker — except, perhaps, under extraordinary circumstances of common peril. And no worker would think of talking to a male; — for males, in this queer world, are inferior beings, equally incapable of fighting or working, and tolerated only as necessary evils. One special class of females—the Mothers-Elect of the race—do condescend to consort with males, during a very brief period, at particular seasons. But the Mothers-Elect do not work; and they *must* accept husbands. A worker could not even dream of keeping company with a male—not merely because such association would signify the most frivolous waste of time, nor yet because the worker necessarily regards all males with unspeakable contempt; but because the worker is incapable of wedlock. Some workers, indeed, are capable of parthenogenesis, and give birth to children who never had fathers. As a general rule, however, the worker is truly feminine by her moral instincts only: she has all the tenderness, the patience, and the foresight that we call "maternal"; but her sex has disappeared, like the sex of the Dragon-Maiden in the Buddhist legend.

For defense against creatures of prey, or enemies of the state, the workers are provided with weapons; and they are furthermore protected by a large military force. The warriors are so much bigger than the workers (in some communities, at least) that it is difficult, at first sight, to believe them of the same race. Soldiers one hundred times larger than the workers whom they guard are not uncommon. But all these soldiers are Amazons—or, more correctly speaking, semi-females. They can work sturdily; but being built for fighting and for heavy pulling chiefly, their usefullness is restricted to those directions in which force, rather than skill, is required.

[Why females, rather than males, should have been evolutionally specialized into soldiery and laborers may not be nearly so simple a question as it appears. I am very sure of not being able to answer it. But natural economy may have decided the matter. In many forms of life, the female greatly exceeds the male in bulk and in energy—perhaps, in this case, the larger reserve of life-force possessed originally by the complete female could be more rapidly and effectively utilized for the development of a special fighting-caste. All energies which, in the fertile female, would be expended in the giving of life seem here to have been diverted to the evolution of aggressive power, or working-capacity.]

Of the true females—the Mothers-Elect—there are very few indeed; and these are treated like queens. So constantly and so reverentially are they waited upon that they can seldom have any wishes to express. They are relieved from every care of existence—except the duty of bearing offspring. Night and day they are cared for in every possible manner. They alone are superabundantly and richly fed:—for the sake of the offspring they must eat and drink and repose right royally; and their physiological specialization allows of such indulgence *ad libitum.* They seldom go out, and never unless attended by a powerful escort; as they cannot be permitted to incur unnecessary fatigue or danger. Probably they have no great desire to go out. Around them revolves the whole activity of the race: all its intelligence and toil and thrift are directed solely toward the well-being of these Mothers and of their children.

But last and least of the race rank the husbands of these Mothers—the necessary Evils—the males. They appear only at a particular season, as I have already observed; and their lives are very short. Some cannot even boast of noble descent, though destined to royal wedlock; for they are not royal offspring, but virgin-born—parthenogenetic children—and, for that reason especially, inferior beings, the chance results of some mysterious atavism. But of any sort of males the commonwealth tolerates but few—barely enough to serve as husbands for the Mothers-Elect, and these few perish almost as soon as their duty has been done. The meaning of Nature's law, in this extraordinary world, is identical with Ruskin's teaching that life without effort is crime; and since the males are useless as workers or fighters, their existence is of only momentary importance. They are not, indeed, sacrified—like the Aztec victim chosen for the festival of Tezcatlipoca, and allowed a honeymoon of twenty days before his heart was torn out. But they are scarcely less unfortunate in their high fortune. Imagine youths brought up in the knowledge that they are destined to become royal bridegrooms for a single night—that after their bridal they will have no moral right to live—that marriage, for each and all of them, will signify certain death—and that they cannot even hope to be lamented by their young widows, who will survive them for a time of many generations. . . . !

V

But all the foregoing is no more than a proem to the real "Romance of the Insect-World".

By far the most startling discovery in relation to this astonishing civilization is that of the suppression of sex. In certain advanced forms of ant-life sex totally disappears in the majority of individuals; in nearly all the higher ant-societies sex-life appears to exist only to the extent absolutely needed for the continuance of the species. But the biological fact in itself is much less startling than the ethical suggestion which it offers—*for this practical suppression, or regulation, of sex-faculty appears to be voluntary!* Voluntary, at least, so far as the species is concerned. It is now believed that these wonderful creatures have learned how to develop, or to arrest the development of, sex in their young by some particular mode of nutrition. They have succeeded in placing under perfect control what is commonly supposed to be the most powerful and unmanageable of instincts. And this rigid restraint of sex-life to within the limits necessary to provide against extinction is but one (though the most amazing) of many vital economies effected by the race. Every capacity for egoistic pleasure—in the common meaning of the word "egoistic"—has been equally repressed through physiological modification. No indulgence of any natural appetite is possible except to that degree in which such indulgence can directly or indirectly benefit the species; even the indispensable requirements of food and sleep being satisfied only to the exact extent necessary for the maintenance of healthy activity. The individual can exist, act, think, only for the communal good; and the commune triumphantly refuses, in so far as cosmic law permits, to let itself be ruled either by Love or Hunger.

Most of us have been brought up in the belief that without some kind of religious creed—some hope of future reward or fear of future punishment—no civilization could exist. We have been taught to think that in the absence of laws based upon moral ideas, and in the absence of an effective police to enforce such laws, nearly everybody would seek only his or her personal advantage, to the disadvantage of everybody else. The strong would then destroy the weak; pity and sympathy would disappear; and the whole social fabric would fall to pieces. . . . These teachings confess the existing imperfection of human nature; and they contain obvious truth. But those who first proclaimed that truth, thousands and thousands of years ago, never imagined a form of social existence in which selfishness would be *naturally* impossible. It remained for irreligious Nature to furnish us with proof positive that there can exist a society in which the pleasure of active beneficence makes needless the idea of duty,—a society in which instinctive morality can dispense with ethical codes of every sort—a society of which every member is born so absolutely unselfish, and so energetically good, that moral training could signify, even for its youngest, neither more nor less than waste of previous time.

To the Evolutionist such facts necessarily suggest that the value of our moral idealism is but temporary; and that something better than virtue, better than kindness, better than self-denial—in the present human meaning of those terms—might, under certain conditions, eventually replace them. He finds himself obliged to face the question whether a world without moral notions might not be morally better than a world in which conduct is regulated by such notions. He must even ask himself whether the existence of religious commandments, moral laws, and ethical standards among ourselves does not prove us still in a very primitive stage of social evolution. And these questions naturally lead up to another: Will humanity ever be able, on this planet, to reach an ethical condition beyond all its ideals—a condition in which everything that we now call evil will have been atrophied out of existence, and everything that we call virtue have been transmuted into instinct—a state of altruism in which ethical concepts and codes will have become as useless as they would be, even now, in the societies of the higher ants.

The giants of modern thought have given some attention to this question; and the greatest among them has answered it—

partly in the affirmative. Herbert Spencer has expressed his belief that humanity will arrive at some state of civilization ethically comparable with that of the ant:

"If we have, in lower orders of creatures, cases in which the nature is constitutionally so modified that altruistic activities have become one with egoistic activities, there is an irresistible implication that a parallel identification will, under parallel conditions, take place among human beings. Social insects furnish us with instances completely to the point—and instances showing us, indeed, to what a marvelous degree the life of the individual may be absorbed in subserving the lives of other individuals. . . . Neither the ant nor the bee can be supposed to have a sense of duty, in the acceptation we give to that word; nor can it be supposed that it is continually undergoing self-sacrifice, in the ordinary acceptation of that word. . . . [The facts] show us that it is within the possibilities of organization to produce a nature which shall be just as energetic and even more energetic in the pursuit of altruistic ends, as is in other cases shown in the pursuit of egoistic ends;—and they show that, in such cases, these altruistic ends are pursued in pursuing ends which, on their other face, are egoistic. For the satisfaction of the needs of the organization, these actions, conducive to the welfare of others, *must* be carried on. . . .

. . . .

"So far from its being true that there must go on, throughout all the future, a condition in which self-regard is to be continually subjected by the regard for others, it will, contrariwise, be the case that a regard for others will eventually become so large a source of pleasure as to overgrow the pleasure which is derivable from direct egoistic gratification. . . . Eventually, then, there will come also a state in which egoism and altruism are so conciliated that the one merges in the other."

VI

Of course the foregoing prediction does not imply that human nature will ever undergo such physiological change as would be represented by structural specializations comparable to those by which the various castes of insect societies are differentiated. We are not bidden to imagine a future state of humanity in which the active majority would consist of semi-female workers and Amazons toiling for an inactive minority of selected Mothers. Even in his chapter, "Human Population in the Future", Mr. Spencer has attempted no detailed statement of the physical modifications inevitable to the production of higher moral types,—though his general statement in regard to a perfected nervous system, and a great diminution of human fertility, suggests that such moral evolution would signify a very considerable amount of physical change. If it be legitimate to believe in a future humanity to which the pleasure of mutual beneficence will represent the whole joy of life, would it not also be legitimate to imagine other transformations, physical and moral, which the facts of insect-biology have proved to be within the range of evolutional possibility? . . . I do not know. I most worshipfully reverence Herbert Spencer as the greatest philosopher that has yet appeared in this world; and I should be very sorry to write down anything contrary to his teaching, in such wise that the reader could imagine it to have been inspired by the Synthetic Philosophy. For the ensuing reflections, I alone am responsible; and if I err, let the sin be upon my own head.

I suppose that the moral transformations predicted by Mr. Spencer could be effected only with the aid of physiological change, and at a terrible cost. Those ethical conditions manifested by insect-societies can have been reached only through effort desperately sustained for millions of years against the most atrocious necessities. Necessities equally merciless may have to be met and mastered eventually by the human race. Mr. Spencer has shown that the time of the greatest possible human suffering is yet to come, and that it will be concomitant with the period of the greatest possible pressure of population. Among other results of that long stress, I understand that there will be a vast increase of human intelligence and sympathy: and that this increase of intelligence will be effected at the cost of human fertility. But this decline in reproductive power will not, we are told, be sufficient to assure the very highest social conditions: it will only relieve that pressure of population which has been the main cause of human suffering. The state of perfect social equilibrium will be approached, but never quite reached, by mankind—

Unless there be discovered some means of solving economic problems, just as social insects have solved them, by the suppression of sex-life.

Supposing that such a discovery were made, and that the human race should decide to arrest the development of sex in the majority of its young—so as to effect a transference of those forces, now demanded by sex-life to the development of higher activities—might not the result be an eventual state of polymorphism, like that of ants? And, in such event, might not the Coming Race be indeed represented in its higher types—through feminine rather than masculine evolution—by a majority of beings of neither sex?

Considering how many persons, even now, through merely unselfish (not to speak of religious) motives, sentence themselves to celibacy, it should not appear improbable that a more highly evolved humanity would cheerfully sacrifice a large proportion of its sex-life for the common weal, particularly in view of certain advantages to be gained. Not the least of such advantages—always supposing that mankind were able to control sex-life after the natural manner of the ants—would be a prodigious increase of longevity. The higher types of a humanity superior to sex might be able to realize the dream of life for a thousand years.

Already we find our lives too short for the work we have to do; and with the constantly accelerating progress of discovery, and the never-ceasing expansion of knowledge, we shall certainly find more and more reason to regret, as time goes on, the brevity of existence. That Science will ever discover the Elixir of the Alchemists' hope is extremely unlikely. The Cosmic

Powers will not allow us to cheat them. For every advantage which they yield us the full price must be paid: nothing for nothing is the everlasting law. Perhaps the price of long life will prove to be the price that the ants have paid for it. Perhaps, upon some elder planet, that price has already been paid, and the power to produce offspring restricted to a caste morphologically differentiated, in unimaginable ways, from the rest of the species. . . .

VII

But while the facts of insect-biology suggest so much in regard to the future course of human evolution, do they not also suggest something of largest significance concerning the relation of ethics to cosmic law? Apparently, the highest evolution will not be permitted to creatures capable of what human moral experience has in all eras condemned. Apparently, the highest possible strength is the strength of unselfishness; and power supreme never will be accorded to cruelty or to lust. There may be no gods; but the forces that shape and dissolve all forms of being would seem to be much more exacting than gods. To prove a "dramatic tendency" in the ways of the stars is not possible; but the cosmic process seems nevertheless to affirm the worth of every human system of ethics fundamentally opposed to human egoism.

A CATALOG OF SELECTED
DOVER BOOKS
IN ALL FIELDS OF INTEREST

A CATALOG OF SELECTED DOVER BOOKS IN ALL FIELDS OF INTEREST

CONCERNING THE SPIRITUAL IN ART, Wassily Kandinsky. Pioneering work by father of abstract art. Thoughts on color theory, nature of art. Analysis of earlier masters. 12 illustrations. 80pp. of text. 5⅜ x 8½. 0-486-23411-8

CELTIC ART: The Methods of Construction, George Bain. Simple geometric techniques for making Celtic interlacements, spirals, Kells-type initials, animals, humans, etc. Over 500 illustrations. 160pp. 9 x 12. (Available in U.S. only.) 0-486-22923-8

AN ATLAS OF ANATOMY FOR ARTISTS, Fritz Schider. Most thorough reference work on art anatomy in the world. Hundreds of illustrations, including selections from works by Vesalius, Leonardo, Goya, Ingres, Michelangelo, others. 593 illustrations. 192pp. 7⅛ x 10¼. 0-486-20241-0

CELTIC HAND STROKE-BY-STROKE (Irish Half-Uncial from "The Book of Kells"): An Arthur Baker Calligraphy Manual, Arthur Baker. Complete guide to creating each letter of the alphabet in distinctive Celtic manner. Covers hand position, strokes, pens, inks, paper, more. Illustrated. 48pp. 8¼ x 11. 0-486-24336-2

EASY ORIGAMI, John Montroll. Charming collection of 32 projects (hat, cup, pelican, piano, swan, many more) specially designed for the novice origami hobbyist. Clearly illustrated easy-to-follow instructions insure that even beginning papercrafters will achieve successful results. 48pp. 8¼ x 11. 0-486-27298-2

BLOOMINGDALE'S ILLUSTRATED 1886 CATALOG: Fashions, Dry Goods and Housewares, Bloomingdale Brothers. Famed merchants' extremely rare catalog depicting about 1,700 products: clothing, housewares, firearms, dry goods, jewelry, more. Invaluable for dating, identifying vintage items. Also, copyright-free graphics for artists, designers. Co-published with Henry Ford Museum & Greenfield Village. 160pp. 8¼ x 11. 0-486-25780-0

THE ART OF WORLDLY WISDOM, Baltasar Gracian. "Think with the few and speak with the many," "Friends are a second existence," and "Be able to forget" are among this 1637 volume's 300 pithy maxims. A perfect source of mental and spiritual refreshment, it can be opened at random and appreciated either in brief or at length. 128pp. 5⅜ x 8½. 0-486-44034-6

JOHNSON'S DICTIONARY: A Modern Selection, Samuel Johnson (E. L. McAdam and George Milne, eds.). This modern version reduces the original 1755 edition's 2,300 pages of definitions and literary examples to a more manageable length, retaining the verbal pleasure and historical curiosity of the original. 480pp. 5 3/16 x 8¼. 0-486-44089-3

ADVENTURES OF HUCKLEBERRY FINN, Mark Twain, Illustrated by E. W. Kemble. A work of eternal richness and complexity, a source of ongoing critical debate, and a literary landmark, Twain's 1885 masterpiece about a barefoot boy's journey of self-discovery has enthralled readers around the world. This handsome clothbound reproduction of the first edition features all 174 of the original black-and-white illustrations. 368pp. 5⅜ x 8½. 0-486-44322-1

STICKLEY CRAFTSMAN FURNITURE CATALOGS, Gustav Stickley and L. & J. G. Stickley. Beautiful, functional furniture in two authentic catalogs from 1910. 594 illustrations, including 277 photos, show settles, rockers, armchairs, reclining chairs, bookcases, desks, tables. 183pp. 6½ x 9¼. 0-486-23838-5

AMERICAN LOCOMOTIVES IN HISTORIC PHOTOGRAPHS: 1858 to 1949, Ron Ziel (ed.). A rare collection of 126 meticulously detailed official photographs, called "builder portraits," of American locomotives that majestically chronicle the rise of steam locomotive power in America. Introduction. Detailed captions. xi+ 129pp. 9 x 12. 0-486-27393-8

AMERICA'S LIGHTHOUSES: An Illustrated History, Francis Ross Holland, Jr. Delightfully written, profusely illustrated fact-filled survey of over 200 American lighthouses since 1716. History, anecdotes, technological advances, more. 240pp. 8 x 10¾. 0-486-25576-X

TOWARDS A NEW ARCHITECTURE, Le Corbusier. Pioneering manifesto by founder of "International School." Technical and aesthetic theories, views of industry, economics, relation of form to function, "mass-production split" and much more. Profusely illustrated. 320pp. 6⅛ x 9¼. (Available in U.S. only.) 0-486-25023-7

HOW THE OTHER HALF LIVES, Jacob Riis. Famous journalistic record, exposing poverty and degradation of New York slums around 1900, by major social reformer. 100 striking and influential photographs. 233pp. 10 x 7⅞. 0-486-22012-5

FRUIT KEY AND TWIG KEY TO TREES AND SHRUBS, William M. Harlow. One of the handiest and most widely used identification aids. Fruit key covers 120 deciduous and evergreen species; twig key 160 deciduous species. Easily used. Over 300 photographs. 126pp. 5⅜ x 8½. 0-486-20511-8

COMMON BIRD SONGS, Dr. Donald J. Borror. Songs of 60 most common U.S. birds: robins, sparrows, cardinals, bluejays, finches, more–arranged in order of increasing complexity. Up to 9 variations of songs of each species. Cassette and manual 0-486-99911-4

ORCHIDS AS HOUSE PLANTS, Rebecca Tyson Northen. Grow cattleyas and many other kinds of orchids–in a window, in a case, or under artificial light. 63 illustrations. 148pp. 5⅜ x 8½. 0-486-23261-1

MONSTER MAZES, Dave Phillips. Masterful mazes at four levels of difficulty. Avoid deadly perils and evil creatures to find magical treasures. Solutions for all 32 exciting illustrated puzzles. 48pp. 8¼ x 11. 0-486-26005-4

MOZART'S DON GIOVANNI (DOVER OPERA LIBRETTO SERIES), Wolfgang Amadeus Mozart. Introduced and translated by Ellen H. Bleiler. Standard Italian libretto, with complete English translation. Convenient and thoroughly portable–an ideal companion for reading along with a recording or the performance itself. Introduction. List of characters. Plot summary. 121pp. 5¼ x 8½. 0-486-24944-1

FRANK LLOYD WRIGHT'S DANA HOUSE, Donald Hoffmann. Pictorial essay of residential masterpiece with over 160 interior and exterior photos, plans, elevations, sketches and studies. 128pp. 9¼ x 10¾. 0-486-29120-0

THE CLARINET AND CLARINET PLAYING, David Pino. Lively, comprehensive work features suggestions about technique, musicianship, and musical interpretation, as well as guidelines for teaching, making your own reeds, and preparing for public performance. Includes an intriguing look at clarinet history. "A godsend," *The Clarinet,* Journal of the International Clarinet Society. Appendixes. 7 illus. 320pp. 5⅜ x 8½. 0-486-40270-3

HOLLYWOOD GLAMOR PORTRAITS, John Kobal (ed.). 145 photos from 1926-49. Harlow, Gable, Bogart, Bacall; 94 stars in all. Full background on photographers, technical aspects. 160pp. 8⅜ x 11¼. 0-486-23352-9

THE RAVEN AND OTHER FAVORITE POEMS, Edgar Allan Poe. Over 40 of the author's most memorable poems: "The Bells," "Ulalume," "Israfel," "To Helen," "The Conqueror Worm," "Eldorado," "Annabel Lee," many more. Alphabetic lists of titles and first lines. 64pp. 5$\frac{3}{16}$ x 8¼. 0-486-26685-0

PERSONAL MEMOIRS OF U. S. GRANT, Ulysses Simpson Grant. Intelligent, deeply moving firsthand account of Civil War campaigns, considered by many the finest military memoirs ever written. Includes letters, historic photographs, maps and more. 528pp. 6⅛ x 9¼. 0-486-28587-1

ANCIENT EGYPTIAN MATERIALS AND INDUSTRIES, A. Lucas and J. Harris. Fascinating, comprehensive, thoroughly documented text describes this ancient civilization's vast resources and the processes that incorporated them in daily life, including the use of animal products, building materials, cosmetics, perfumes and incense, fibers, glazed ware, glass and its manufacture, materials used in the mummification process, and much more. 544pp. 6⅛ x 9¼. (Available in U.S. only.) 0-486-40446-3

RUSSIAN STORIES/RUSSKIE RASSKAZY: A Dual-Language Book, edited by Gleb Struve. Twelve tales by such masters as Chekhov, Tolstoy, Dostoevsky, Pushkin, others. Excellent word-for-word English translations on facing pages, plus teaching and study aids, Russian/English vocabulary, biographical/critical introductions, more. 416pp. 5⅜ x 8½. 0-486-26244-8

PHILADELPHIA THEN AND NOW: 60 Sites Photographed in the Past and Present, Kenneth Finkel and Susan Oyama. Rare photographs of City Hall, Logan Square, Independence Hall, Betsy Ross House, other landmarks juxtaposed with contemporary views. Captures changing face of historic city. Introduction. Captions. 128pp. 8¼ x 11. 0-486-25790-8

NORTH AMERICAN INDIAN LIFE: Customs and Traditions of 23 Tribes, Elsie Clews Parsons (ed.). 27 fictionalized essays by noted anthropologists examine religion, customs, government, additional facets of life among the Winnebago, Crow, Zuni, Eskimo, other tribes. 480pp. 6⅛ x 9¼. 0-486-27377-6

TECHNICAL MANUAL AND DICTIONARY OF CLASSICAL BALLET, Gail Grant. Defines, explains, comments on steps, movements, poses and concepts. 15-page pictorial section. Basic book for student, viewer. 127pp. 5⅜ x 8½. 0-486-21843-0

THE MALE AND FEMALE FIGURE IN MOTION: 60 Classic Photographic Sequences, Eadweard Muybridge. 60 true-action photographs of men and women walking, running, climbing, bending, turning, etc., reproduced from rare 19th-century masterpiece. vi + 121pp. 9 x 12. 0-486-24745-7

CATALOG OF DOVER BOOKS

ANIMALS: 1,419 Copyright-Free Illustrations of Mammals, Birds, Fish, Insects, etc., Jim Harter (ed.). Clear wood engravings present, in extremely lifelike poses, over 1,000 species of animals. One of the most extensive pictorial sourcebooks of its kind. Captions. Index. 284pp. 9 x 12. 0-486-23766-4

1001 QUESTIONS ANSWERED ABOUT THE SEASHORE, N. J. Berrill and Jacquelyn Berrill. Queries answered about dolphins, sea snails, sponges, starfish, fishes, shore birds, many others. Covers appearance, breeding, growth, feeding, much more. 305pp. 5¼ x 8¼. 0-486-23366-9

ATTRACTING BIRDS TO YOUR YARD, William J. Weber. Easy-to-follow guide offers advice on how to attract the greatest diversity of birds: birdhouses, feeders, water and waterers, much more. 96pp. 5$\frac{3}{16}$ x 8¼. 0-486-28927-3

MEDICINAL AND OTHER USES OF NORTH AMERICAN PLANTS: A Historical Survey with Special Reference to the Eastern Indian Tribes, Charlotte Erichsen-Brown. Chronological historical citations document 500 years of usage of plants, trees, shrubs native to eastern Canada, northeastern U.S. Also complete identifying information. 343 illustrations. 544pp. 6½ x 9¼. 0-486-25951-X

STORYBOOK MAZES, Dave Phillips. 23 stories and mazes on two-page spreads: Wizard of Oz, Treasure Island, Robin Hood, etc. Solutions. 64pp. 8¼ x 11. 0-486-23628-5

AMERICAN NEGRO SONGS: 230 Folk Songs and Spirituals, Religious and Secular, John W. Work. This authoritative study traces the African influences of songs sung and played by black Americans at work, in church, and as entertainment. The author discusses the lyric significance of such songs as "Swing Low, Sweet Chariot," "John Henry," and others and offers the words and music for 230 songs. Bibliography. Index of Song Titles. 272pp. 6½ x 9¼. 0-486-40271-1

MOVIE-STAR PORTRAITS OF THE FORTIES, John Kobal (ed.). 163 glamor, studio photos of 106 stars of the 1940s: Rita Hayworth, Ava Gardner, Marlon Brando, Clark Gable, many more. 176pp. 8⅜ x 11¼. 0-486-23546-7

YEKL and THE IMPORTED BRIDEGROOM AND OTHER STORIES OF YIDDISH NEW YORK, Abraham Cahan. Film Hester Street based on *Yekl* (1896). Novel, other stories among first about Jewish immigrants on N.Y.'s East Side. 240pp. 5⅜ x 8½. 0-486-22427-9

SELECTED POEMS, Walt Whitman. Generous sampling from *Leaves of Grass*. Twenty-four poems include "I Hear America Singing," "Song of the Open Road," "I Sing the Body Electric," "When Lilacs Last in the Dooryard Bloom'd," "O Captain! My Captain!"–all reprinted from an authoritative edition. Lists of titles and first lines. 128pp. 5$\frac{3}{16}$ x 8¼. 0-486-26878-0

SONGS OF EXPERIENCE: Facsimile Reproduction with 26 Plates in Full Color, William Blake. 26 full-color plates from a rare 1826 edition. Includes "The Tyger," "London," "Holy Thursday," and other poems. Printed text of poems. 48pp. 5¼ x 7. 0-486-24636-1

THE BEST TALES OF HOFFMANN, E. T. A. Hoffmann. 10 of Hoffmann's most important stories: "Nutcracker and the King of Mice," "The Golden Flowerpot," etc. 458pp. 5⅜ x 8½. 0-486-21793-0

THE BOOK OF TEA, Kakuzo Okakura. Minor classic of the Orient: entertaining, charming explanation, interpretation of traditional Japanese culture in terms of tea ceremony. 94pp. 5⅜ x 8½. 0-486-20070-1

FRENCH STORIES/CONTES FRANÇAIS: A Dual-Language Book, Wallace Fowlie. Ten stories by French masters, Voltaire to Camus: "Micromegas" by Voltaire; "The Atheist's Mass" by Balzac; "Minuet" by de Maupassant; "The Guest" by Camus, six more. Excellent English translations on facing pages. Also French-English vocabulary list, exercises, more. 352pp. 5⅜ x 8½. 0-486-26443-2

CHICAGO AT THE TURN OF THE CENTURY IN PHOTOGRAPHS: 122 Historic Views from the Collections of the Chicago Historical Society, Larry A. Viskochil. Rare large-format prints offer detailed views of City Hall, State Street, the Loop, Hull House, Union Station, many other landmarks, circa 1904-1913. Introduction. Captions. Maps. 144pp. 9⅜ x 12¼. 0-486-24656-6

OLD BROOKLYN IN EARLY PHOTOGRAPHS, 1865-1929, William Lee Younger. Luna Park, Gravesend race track, construction of Grand Army Plaza, moving of Hotel Brighton, etc. 157 previously unpublished photographs. 165pp. 8⅞ x 11¾. 0-486-23587-4

THE MYTHS OF THE NORTH AMERICAN INDIANS, Lewis Spence. Rich anthology of the myths and legends of the Algonquins, Iroquois, Pawnees and Sioux, prefaced by an extensive historical and ethnological commentary. 36 illustrations. 480pp. 5⅜ x 8½. 0-486-25967-6

AN ENCYCLOPEDIA OF BATTLES: Accounts of Over 1,560 Battles from 1479 B.C. to the Present, David Eggenberger. Essential details of every major battle in recorded history from the first battle of Megiddo in 1479 B.C. to Grenada in 1984. List of Battle Maps. New Appendix covering the years 1967-1984. Index. 99 illustrations. 544pp. 6½ x 9¼. 0-486-24913-1

SAILING ALONE AROUND THE WORLD, Captain Joshua Slocum. First man to sail around the world, alone, in small boat. One of great feats of seamanship told in delightful manner. 67 illustrations. 294pp. 5⅜ x 8½. 0-486-20326-3

ANARCHISM AND OTHER ESSAYS, Emma Goldman. Powerful, penetrating, prophetic essays on direct action, role of minorities, prison reform, puritan hypocrisy, violence, etc. 271pp. 5⅜ x 8½. 0-486-22484-8

MYTHS OF THE HINDUS AND BUDDHISTS, Ananda K. Coomaraswamy and Sister Nivedita. Great stories of the epics; deeds of Krishna, Shiva, taken from puranas, Vedas, folk tales; etc. 32 illustrations. 400pp. 5⅜ x 8½. 0-486-21759-0

MY BONDAGE AND MY FREEDOM, Frederick Douglass. Born a slave, Douglass became outspoken force in antislavery movement. The best of Douglass' autobiographies. Graphic description of slave life. 464pp. 5⅜ x 8½. 0-486-22457-0

FOLLOWING THE EQUATOR: A Journey Around the World, Mark Twain. Fascinating humorous account of 1897 voyage to Hawaii, Australia, India, New Zealand, etc. Ironic, bemused reports on peoples, customs, climate, flora and fauna, politics, much more. 197 illustrations. 720pp. 5⅜ x 8½. 0-486-26113-1

THE PEOPLE CALLED SHAKERS, Edward D. Andrews. Definitive study of Shakers: origins, beliefs, practices, dances, social organization, furniture and crafts, etc. 33 illustrations. 351pp. 5⅜ x 8½. 0-486-21081-2

THE MYTHS OF GREECE AND ROME, H. A. Guerber. A classic of mythology, generously illustrated, long prized for its simple, graphic, accurate retelling of the principal myths of Greece and Rome, and for its commentary on their origins and significance. With 64 illustrations by Michelangelo, Raphael, Titian, Rubens, Canova, Bernini and others. 480pp. 5⅜ x 8½. 0-486-27584-1

PSYCHOLOGY OF MUSIC, Carl E. Seashore. Classic work discusses music as a medium from psychological viewpoint. Clear treatment of physical acoustics, auditory apparatus, sound perception, development of musical skills, nature of musical feeling, host of other topics. 88 figures. 408pp. 5⅜ x 8½. 0-486-21851-1

LIFE IN ANCIENT EGYPT, Adolf Erman. Fullest, most thorough, detailed older account with much not in more recent books, domestic life, religion, magic, medicine, commerce, much more. Many illustrations reproduce tomb paintings, carvings, hieroglyphs, etc. 597pp. 5⅜ x 8½. 0-486-22632-8

SUNDIALS, Their Theory and Construction, Albert Waugh. Far and away the best, most thorough coverage of ideas, mathematics concerned, types, construction, adjusting anywhere. Simple, nontechnical treatment allows even children to build several of these dials. Over 100 illustrations. 230pp. 5⅜ x 8½. 0-486-22947-5

THEORETICAL HYDRODYNAMICS, L. M. Milne-Thomson. Classic exposition of the mathematical theory of fluid motion, applicable to both hydrodynamics and aerodynamics. Over 600 exercises. 768pp. 6⅛ x 9¼. 0-486-68970-0

OLD-TIME VIGNETTES IN FULL COLOR, Carol Belanger Grafton (ed.). Over 390 charming, often sentimental illustrations, selected from archives of Victorian graphics–pretty women posing, children playing, food, flowers, kittens and puppies, smiling cherubs, birds and butterflies, much more. All copyright-free. 48pp. 9¼ x 12¼. 0-486-27269-9

PERSPECTIVE FOR ARTISTS, Rex Vicat Cole. Depth, perspective of sky and sea, shadows, much more, not usually covered. 391 diagrams, 81 reproductions of drawings and paintings. 279pp. 5⅜ x 8½. 0-486-22487-2

DRAWING THE LIVING FIGURE, Joseph Sheppard. Innovative approach to artistic anatomy focuses on specifics of surface anatomy, rather than muscles and bones. Over 170 drawings of live models in front, back and side views, and in widely varying poses. Accompanying diagrams. 177 illustrations. Introduction. Index. 144pp. 8⅜ x11¼. 0-486-26723-7

GOTHIC AND OLD ENGLISH ALPHABETS: 100 Complete Fonts, Dan X. Solo. Add power, elegance to posters, signs, other graphics with 100 stunning copyright-free alphabets: Blackstone, Dolbey, Germania, 97 more–including many lower-case, numerals, punctuation marks. 104pp. 8⅛ x 11. 0-486-24695-7

THE BOOK OF WOOD CARVING, Charles Marshall Sayers. Finest book for beginners discusses fundamentals and offers 34 designs. "Absolutely first rate . . . well thought out and well executed."–E. J. Tangerman. 118pp. 7¾ x 10⅝. 0-486-23654-4

ILLUSTRATED CATALOG OF CIVIL WAR MILITARY GOODS: Union Army Weapons, Insignia, Uniform Accessories, and Other Equipment, Schuyler, Hartley, and Graham. Rare, profusely illustrated 1846 catalog includes Union Army uniform and dress regulations, arms and ammunition, coats, insignia, flags, swords, rifles, etc. 226 illustrations. 160pp. 9 x 12. 0-486-24939-5

WOMEN'S FASHIONS OF THE EARLY 1900s: An Unabridged Republication of "New York Fashions, 1909," National Cloak & Suit Co. Rare catalog of mail-order fashions documents women's and children's clothing styles shortly after the turn of the century. Captions offer full descriptions, prices. Invaluable resource for fashion, costume historians. Approximately 725 illustrations. 128pp. 8⅜ x 11¼. 0-486-27276-1

HOW TO DO BEADWORK, Mary White. Fundamental book on craft from simple projects to five-bead chains and woven works. 106 illustrations. 142pp. $5\frac{3}{8}$ x 8.
0-486-20697-1

THE 1912 AND 1915 GUSTAV STICKLEY FURNITURE CATALOGS, Gustav Stickley. With over 200 detailed illustrations and descriptions, these two catalogs are essential reading and reference materials and identification guides for Stickley furniture. Captions cite materials, dimensions and prices. 112pp. $6\frac{1}{2}$ x $9\frac{1}{4}$. 0-486-26676-1

EARLY AMERICAN LOCOMOTIVES, John H. White, Jr. Finest locomotive engravings from early 19th century: historical (1804–74), main-line (after 1870), special, foreign, etc. 147 plates. 142pp. $11\frac{3}{8}$ x $8\frac{1}{4}$. 0-486-22772-3

LITTLE BOOK OF EARLY AMERICAN CRAFTS AND TRADES, Peter Stockham (ed.). 1807 children's book explains crafts and trades: baker, hatter, cooper, potter, and many others. 23 copperplate illustrations. 140pp. $4\frac{5}{8}$ x 6.
0-486-23336-7

VICTORIAN FASHIONS AND COSTUMES FROM HARPER'S BAZAR, 1867–1898, Stella Blum (ed.). Day costumes, evening wear, sports clothes, shoes, hats, other accessories in over 1,000 detailed engravings. 320pp. $9\frac{3}{8}$ x $12\frac{1}{4}$.
0-486-22990-4

THE LONG ISLAND RAIL ROAD IN EARLY PHOTOGRAPHS, Ron Ziel. Over 220 rare photos, informative text document origin (1844) and development of rail service on Long Island. Vintage views of early trains, locomotives, stations, passengers, crews, much more. Captions. $8\frac{7}{8}$ x $11\frac{3}{4}$. 0-486-26301-0

VOYAGE OF THE LIBERDADE, Joshua Slocum. Great 19th-century mariner's thrilling, first-hand account of the wreck of his ship off South America, the 35-foot boat he built from the wreckage, and its remarkable voyage home. 128pp. $5\frac{3}{8}$ x $8\frac{1}{2}$.
0-486-40022-0

TEN BOOKS ON ARCHITECTURE, Vitruvius. The most important book ever written on architecture. Early Roman aesthetics, technology, classical orders, site selection, all other aspects. Morgan translation. 331pp. $5\frac{3}{8}$ x $8\frac{1}{2}$. 0-486-20645-9

THE HUMAN FIGURE IN MOTION, Eadweard Muybridge. More than 4,500 stopped-action photos, in action series, showing undraped men, women, children jumping, lying down, throwing, sitting, wrestling, carrying, etc. 390pp. $7\frac{7}{8}$ x $10\frac{5}{8}$.
0-486-20204-6 Clothbd.

TREES OF THE EASTERN AND CENTRAL UNITED STATES AND CANADA, William M. Harlow. Best one-volume guide to 140 trees. Full descriptions, woodlore, range, etc. Over 600 illustrations. Handy size. 288pp. $4\frac{1}{2}$ x $6\frac{3}{8}$. 0-486-20395-6

GROWING AND USING HERBS AND SPICES, Milo Miloradovich. Versatile handbook provides all the information needed for cultivation and use of all the herbs and spices available in North America. 4 illustrations. Index. Glossary. 236pp. $5\frac{3}{8}$ x $8\frac{1}{2}$.
0-486-25058-X

BIG BOOK OF MAZES AND LABYRINTHS, Walter Shepherd. 50 mazes and labyrinths in all–classical, solid, ripple, and more–in one great volume. Perfect inexpensive puzzler for clever youngsters. Full solutions. 112pp. $8\frac{1}{8}$ x 11. 0-486-22951-3

PIANO TUNING, J. Cree Fischer. Clearest, best book for beginner, amateur. Simple repairs, raising dropped notes, tuning by easy method of flattened fifths. No previous skills needed. 4 illustrations. 201pp. $5\frac{3}{8}$ x $8\frac{1}{2}$. 0-486-23267-0

DRIED FLOWERS: How to Prepare Them, Sarah Whitlock and Martha Rankin. Complete instructions on how to use silica gel, meal and borax, perlite aggregate, sand and borax, glycerine and water to create attractive permanent flower arrangements. 12 illustrations. 32pp. 5⅜ x 8½. 0-486-21802-3

EASY-TO-MAKE BIRD FEEDERS FOR WOODWORKERS, Scott D. Campbell. Detailed, simple-to-use guide for designing, constructing, caring for and using feeders. Text, illustrations for 12 classic and contemporary designs. 96pp. 5⅜ x 8½. 0-486-25847-5

THE COMPLETE BOOK OF BIRDHOUSE CONSTRUCTION FOR WOODWORKERS, Scott D. Campbell. Detailed instructions, illustrations, tables. Also data on bird habitat and instinct patterns. Bibliography. 3 tables. 63 illustrations in 15 figures. 48pp. 5¼ x 8½. 0-486-24407-5

SCOTTISH WONDER TALES FROM MYTH AND LEGEND, Donald A. Mackenzie. 16 lively tales tell of giants rumbling down mountainsides, of a magic wand that turns stone pillars into warriors, of gods and goddesses, evil hags, powerful forces and more. 240pp. 5⅜ x 8½. 0-486-29677-6

THE HISTORY OF UNDERCLOTHES, C. Willett Cunnington and Phyllis Cunnington. Fascinating, well-documented survey covering six centuries of English undergarments, enhanced with over 100 illustrations: 12th-century laced-up bodice, footed long drawers (1795), 19th-century bustles, 19th-century corsets for men, Victorian "bust improvers," much more. 272pp. 5⅜ x 8¼. 0-486-27124-2

ARTS AND CRAFTS FURNITURE: The Complete Brooks Catalog of 1912, Brooks Manufacturing Co. Photos and detailed descriptions of more than 150 now very collectible furniture designs from the Arts and Crafts movement depict davenports, settees, buffets, desks, tables, chairs, bedsteads, dressers and more, all built of solid, quarter-sawed oak. Invaluable for students and enthusiasts of antiques, Americana and the decorative arts. 80pp. 6½ x 9¼. 0-486-27471-3

WILBUR AND ORVILLE: A Biography of the Wright Brothers, Fred Howard. Definitive, crisply written study tells the full story of the brothers' lives and work. A vividly written biography, unparalleled in scope and color, that also captures the spirit of an extraordinary era. 560pp. 6⅛ x 9¼. 0-486-40297-5

THE ARTS OF THE SAILOR: Knotting, Splicing and Ropework, Hervey Garrett Smith. Indispensable shipboard reference covers tools, basic knots and useful hitches; handsewing and canvas work, more. Over 100 illustrations. Delightful reading for sea lovers. 256pp. 5⅜ x 8½. 0-486-26440-8

FRANK LLOYD WRIGHT'S FALLINGWATER: The House and Its History, Second, Revised Edition, Donald Hoffmann. A total revision–both in text and illustrations–of the standard document on Fallingwater, the boldest, most personal architectural statement of Wright's mature years, updated with valuable new material from the recently opened Frank Lloyd Wright Archives. "Fascinating"–*The New York Times*. 116 illustrations. 128pp. 9¼ x 10¾. 0-486-27430-6

PHOTOGRAPHIC SKETCHBOOK OF THE CIVIL WAR, Alexander Gardner. 100 photos taken on field during the Civil War. Famous shots of Manassas Harper's Ferry, Lincoln, Richmond, slave pens, etc. 244pp. 10⅞ x 8¼. 0-486-22731-6

FIVE ACRES AND INDEPENDENCE, Maurice G. Kains. Great back-to-the-land classic explains basics of self-sufficient farming. The one book to get. 95 illustrations. 397pp. 5⅜ x 8½. 0-486-20974-1

A MODERN HERBAL, Margaret Grieve. Much the fullest, most exact, most useful compilation of herbal material. Gigantic alphabetical encyclopedia, from aconite to zedoary, gives botanical information, medical properties, folklore, economic uses, much else. Indispensable to serious reader. 161 illustrations. 888pp. 6½ x 9¼. 2-vol. set. (Available in U.S. only.) Vol. I: 0-486-22798-7 Vol. II: 0-486-22799-5

HIDDEN TREASURE MAZE BOOK, Dave Phillips. Solve 34 challenging mazes accompanied by heroic tales of adventure. Evil dragons, people-eating plants, blood-thirsty giants, many more dangerous adversaries lurk at every twist and turn. 34 mazes, stories, solutions. 48pp. 8¼ x 11. 0-486-24566-7

LETTERS OF W. A. MOZART, Wolfgang A. Mozart. Remarkable letters show bawdy wit, humor, imagination, musical insights, contemporary musical world; includes some letters from Leopold Mozart. 276pp. 5⅜ x 8½. 0-486-22859-2

BASIC PRINCIPLES OF CLASSICAL BALLET, Agrippina Vaganova. Great Russian theoretician, teacher explains methods for teaching classical ballet. 118 illustrations. 175pp. 5⅜ x 8½. 0-486-22036-2

THE JUMPING FROG, Mark Twain. Revenge edition. The original story of The Celebrated Jumping Frog of Calaveras County, a hapless French translation, and Twain's hilarious "retranslation" from the French. 12 illustrations. 66pp. 5⅜ x 8½. 0-486-22686-7

BEST REMEMBERED POEMS, Martin Gardner (ed.). The 126 poems in this superb collection of 19th- and 20th-century British and American verse range from Shelley's "To a Skylark" to the impassioned "Renascence" of Edna St. Vincent Millay and to Edward Lear's whimsical "The Owl and the Pussycat." 224pp. 5⅜ x 8½. 0-486-27165-X

COMPLETE SONNETS, William Shakespeare. Over 150 exquisite poems deal with love, friendship, the tyranny of time, beauty's evanescence, death and other themes in language of remarkable power, precision and beauty. Glossary of archaic terms. 80pp. 5³⁄₁₆ x 8¼. 0-486-26686-9

HISTORIC HOMES OF THE AMERICAN PRESIDENTS, Second, Revised Edition, Irvin Haas. A traveler's guide to American Presidential homes, most open to the public, depicting and describing homes occupied by every American President from George Washington to George Bush. With visiting hours, admission charges, travel routes. 175 photographs. Index. 160pp. 8¼ x 11. 0-486-26751-2

THE WIT AND HUMOR OF OSCAR WILDE, Alvin Redman (ed.). More than 1,000 ripostes, paradoxes, wisecracks: Work is the curse of the drinking classes; I can resist everything except temptation; etc. 258pp. 5⅜ x 8½. 0-486-20602-5

SHAKESPEARE LEXICON AND QUOTATION DICTIONARY, Alexander Schmidt. Full definitions, locations, shades of meaning in every word in plays and poems. More than 50,000 exact quotations. 1,485pp. 6½ x 9¼. 2-vol. set. Vol. 1: 0-486-22726-X Vol. 2: 0-486-22727-8

SELECTED POEMS, Emily Dickinson. Over 100 best-known, best-loved poems by one of America's foremost poets, reprinted from authoritative early editions. No comparable edition at this price. Index of first lines. 64pp. 5³⁄₁₆ x 8¼. 0-486-26466-1

THE INSIDIOUS DR. FU-MANCHU, Sax Rohmer. The first of the popular mystery series introduces a pair of English detectives to their archnemesis, the diabolical Dr. Fu-Manchu. Flavorful atmosphere, fast-paced action, and colorful characters enliven this classic of the genre. 208pp. 5³⁄₁₆ x 8¼. 0-486-29898-1

THE MALLEUS MALEFICARUM OF KRAMER AND SPRENGER, translated by Montague Summers. Full text of most important witchhunter's "bible," used by both Catholics and Protestants. 278pp. 6⅝ x 10. 0-486-22802-9

SPANISH STORIES/CUENTOS ESPAÑOLES: A Dual-Language Book, Angel Flores (ed.). Unique format offers 13 great stories in Spanish by Cervantes, Borges, others. Faithful English translations on facing pages. 352pp. 5⅜ x 8½. 0-486-25399-6

GARDEN CITY, LONG ISLAND, IN EARLY PHOTOGRAPHS, 1869–1919, Mildred H. Smith. Handsome treasury of 118 vintage pictures, accompanied by carefully researched captions, document the Garden City Hotel fire (1899), the Vanderbilt Cup Race (1908), the first airmail flight departing from the Nassau Boulevard Aerodrome (1911), and much more. 96pp. 8⅞ x 11¾. 0-486-40669-5

OLD QUEENS, N.Y., IN EARLY PHOTOGRAPHS, Vincent F. Seyfried and William Asadorian. Over 160 rare photographs of Maspeth, Jamaica, Jackson Heights, and other areas. Vintage views of DeWitt Clinton mansion, 1939 World's Fair and more. Captions. 192pp. 8⅞ x 11. 0-486-26358-4

CAPTURED BY THE INDIANS: 15 Firsthand Accounts, 1750-1870, Frederick Drimmer. Astounding true historical accounts of grisly torture, bloody conflicts, relentless pursuits, miraculous escapes and more, by people who lived to tell the tale. 384pp. 5⅜ x 8½. 0-486-24901-8

THE WORLD'S GREAT SPEECHES (Fourth Enlarged Edition), Lewis Copeland, Lawrence W. Lamm, and Stephen J. McKenna. Nearly 300 speeches provide public speakers with a wealth of updated quotes and inspiration–from Pericles' funeral oration and William Jennings Bryan's "Cross of Gold Speech" to Malcolm X's powerful words on the Black Revolution and Earl of Spenser's tribute to his sister, Diana, Princess of Wales. 944pp. 5⅜ x 8⅜. 0-486-40903-1

THE BOOK OF THE SWORD, Sir Richard F. Burton. Great Victorian scholar/adventurer's eloquent, erudite history of the "queen of weapons"–from prehistory to early Roman Empire. Evolution and development of early swords, variations (sabre, broadsword, cutlass, scimitar, etc.), much more. 336pp. 6⅛ x 9¼. 0-486-25434-8

AUTOBIOGRAPHY: The Story of My Experiments with Truth, Mohandas K. Gandhi. Boyhood, legal studies, purification, the growth of the Satyagraha (nonviolent protest) movement. Critical, inspiring work of the man responsible for the freedom of India. 480pp. 5⅜ x 8½. (Available in U.S. only.) 0-486-24593-4

CELTIC MYTHS AND LEGENDS, T. W. Rolleston. Masterful retelling of Irish and Welsh stories and tales. Cuchulain, King Arthur, Deirdre, the Grail, many more. First paperback edition. 58 full-page illustrations. 512pp. 5⅜ x 8½. 0-486-26507-2

THE PRINCIPLES OF PSYCHOLOGY, William James. Famous long course complete, unabridged. Stream of thought, time perception, memory, experimental methods; great work decades ahead of its time. 94 figures. 1,391pp. 5⅜ x 8½. 2-vol. set.
Vol. I: 0-486-20381-6 Vol. II: 0-486-20382-4

THE WORLD AS WILL AND REPRESENTATION, Arthur Schopenhauer. Definitive English translation of Schopenhauer's life work, correcting more than 1,000 errors, omissions in earlier translations. Translated by E. F. J. Payne. Total of 1,269pp. 5⅜ x 8½. 2-vol. set. Vol. 1: 0-486-21761-2 Vol. 2: 0-486-21762-0

MAGIC AND MYSTERY IN TIBET, Madame Alexandra David-Neel. Experiences among lamas, magicians, sages, sorcerers, Bonpa wizards. A true psychic discovery. 32 illustrations. 321pp. 5⅜ x 8½. (Available in U.S. only.) 0-486-22682-4

THE EGYPTIAN BOOK OF THE DEAD, E. A. Wallis Budge. Complete reproduction of Ani's papyrus, finest ever found. Full hieroglyphic text, interlinear transliteration, word-for-word translation, smooth translation. 533pp. 6½ x 9¼. 0-486-21866-X

HISTORIC COSTUME IN PICTURES, Braun & Schneider. Over 1,450 costumed figures in clearly detailed engravings–from dawn of civilization to end of 19th century. Captions. Many folk costumes. 256pp. 8⅜ x 11¾. 0-486-23150-X

MATHEMATICS FOR THE NONMATHEMATICIAN, Morris Kline. Detailed, college-level treatment of mathematics in cultural and historical context, with numerous exercises. Recommended Reading Lists. Tables. Numerous figures. 641pp. 5⅜ x 8½. 0-486-24823-2

PROBABILISTIC METHODS IN THE THEORY OF STRUCTURES, Isaac Elishakoff. Well-written introduction covers the elements of the theory of probability from two or more random variables, the reliability of such multivariable structures, the theory of random function, Monte Carlo methods of treating problems incapable of exact solution, and more. Examples. 502pp. 5⅜ x 8½. 0-486-40691-1

THE RIME OF THE ANCIENT MARINER, Gustave Doré, S. T. Coleridge. Doré's finest work; 34 plates capture moods, subtleties of poem. Flawless full-size reproductions printed on facing pages with authoritative text of poem. "Beautiful. Simply beautiful."–*Publisher's Weekly*. 77pp. 9¼ x 12. 0-486-22305-1

SCULPTURE: Principles and Practice, Louis Slobodkin. Step-by-step approach to clay, plaster, metals, stone; classical and modern. 253 drawings, photos. 255pp. 8⅛ x 11. 0-486-22960-2

THE INFLUENCE OF SEA POWER UPON HISTORY, 1660–1783, A. T. Mahan. Influential classic of naval history and tactics still used as text in war colleges. First paperback edition. 4 maps. 24 battle plans. 640pp. 5⅜ x 8½. 0-486-25509-3

THE STORY OF THE TITANIC AS TOLD BY ITS SURVIVORS, Jack Winocour (ed.). What it was really like. Panic, despair, shocking inefficiency, and a little heroism. More thrilling than any fictional account. 26 illustrations. 320pp. 5⅜ x 8½. 0-486-20610-6

ONE TWO THREE . . . INFINITY: Facts and Speculations of Science, George Gamow. Great physicist's fascinating, readable overview of contemporary science: number theory, relativity, fourth dimension, entropy, genes, atomic structure, much more. 128 illustrations. Index. 352pp. 5⅜ x 8½. 0-486-25664-2

DALÍ ON MODERN ART: The Cuckolds of Antiquated Modern Art, Salvador Dalí. Influential painter skewers modern art and its practitioners. Outrageous evaluations of Picasso, Cézanne, Turner, more. 15 renderings of paintings discussed. 44 calligraphic decorations by Dalí. 96pp. 5⅜ x 8½. (Available in U.S. only.) 0-486-29220-7

ANTIQUE PLAYING CARDS: A Pictorial History, Henry René D'Allemagne. Over 900 elaborate, decorative images from rare playing cards (14th–20th centuries): Bacchus, death, dancing dogs, hunting scenes, royal coats of arms, players cheating, much more. 96pp. 9¼ x 12¼. 0-486-29265-7

CATALOG OF DOVER BOOKS

MAKING FURNITURE MASTERPIECES: 30 Projects with Measured Drawings, Franklin H. Gottshall. Step-by-step instructions, illustrations for constructing handsome, useful pieces, among them a Sheraton desk, Chippendale chair, Spanish desk, Queen Anne table and a William and Mary dressing mirror. 224pp. 8⅛ x 11¼. 0-486-29338-6

NORTH AMERICAN INDIAN DESIGNS FOR ARTISTS AND CRAFTSPEOPLE, Eva Wilson. Over 360 authentic copyright-free designs adapted from Navajo blankets, Hopi pottery, Sioux buffalo hides, more. Geometrics, symbolic figures, plant and animal motifs, etc. 128pp. 8⅜ x 11. (Not for sale in the United Kingdom.) 0-486-25341-4

THE FOSSIL BOOK: A Record of Prehistoric Life, Patricia V. Rich et al. Profusely illustrated definitive guide covers everything from single-celled organisms and dinosaurs to birds and mammals and the interplay between climate and man. Over 1,500 illustrations. 760pp. 7½ x 10⅛. 0-486-29371-8

VICTORIAN ARCHITECTURAL DETAILS: Designs for Over 700 Stairs, Mantels, Doors, Windows, Cornices, Porches, and Other Decorative Elements, A. J. Bicknell & Company. Everything from dormer windows and piazzas to balconies and gable ornaments. Also includes elevations and floor plans for handsome, private residences and commercial structures. 80pp. 9⅜ x 12¼. 0-486-44015-X

WESTERN ISLAMIC ARCHITECTURE: A Concise Introduction, John D. Hoag. Profusely illustrated critical appraisal compares and contrasts Islamic mosques and palaces–from Spain and Egypt to other areas in the Middle East. 139 illustrations. 128pp. 6 x 9. 0-486-43760-4

CHINESE ARCHITECTURE: A Pictorial History, Liang Ssu-ch'eng. More than 240 rare photographs and drawings depict temples, pagodas, tombs, bridges, and imperial palaces comprising much of China's architectural heritage. 152 halftones, 94 diagrams. 232pp. 10¾ x 9⅞. 0-486-43999-2

THE RENAISSANCE: Studies in Art and Poetry, Walter Pater. One of the most talked-about books of the 19th century, *The Renaissance* combines scholarship and philosophy in an innovative work of cultural criticism that examines the achievements of Botticelli, Leonardo, Michelangelo, and other artists. "The holy writ of beauty."–Oscar Wilde. 160pp. 5⅜ x 8½. 0-486-44025-7

A TREATISE ON PAINTING, Leonardo da Vinci. The great Renaissance artist's practical advice on drawing and painting techniques covers anatomy, perspective, composition, light and shadow, and color. A classic of art instruction, it features 48 drawings by Nicholas Poussin and Leon Battista Alberti. 192pp. 5⅜ x 8½. 0-486-44155-5

THE MIND OF LEONARDO DA VINCI, Edward McCurdy. More than just a biography, this classic study by a distinguished historian draws upon Leonardo's extensive writings to offer numerous demonstrations of the Renaissance master's achievements, not only in sculpture and painting, but also in music, engineering, and even experimental aviation. 384pp. 5⅜ x 8½. 0-486-44142-3

WASHINGTON IRVING'S RIP VAN WINKLE, Illustrated by Arthur Rackham. Lovely prints that established artist as a leading illustrator of the time and forever etched into the popular imagination a classic of Catskill lore. 51 full-color plates. 80pp. 8⅜ x 11. 0-486-44242-X

HENSCHE ON PAINTING, John W. Robichaux. Basic painting philosophy and methodology of a great teacher, as expounded in his famous classes and workshops on Cape Cod. 7 illustrations in color on covers. 80pp. 5⅜ x 8½. 0-486-43728-0

CATALOG OF DOVER BOOKS

LIGHT AND SHADE: A Classic Approach to Three-Dimensional Drawing, Mrs. Mary P. Merrifield. Handy reference clearly demonstrates principles of light and shade by revealing effects of common daylight, sunshine, and candle or artificial light on geometrical solids. 13 plates. 64pp. 5⅜ x 8½. 0-486-44143-1

ASTROLOGY AND ASTRONOMY: A Pictorial Archive of Signs and Symbols, Ernst and Johanna Lehner. Treasure trove of stories, lore, and myth, accompanied by more than 300 rare illustrations of planets, the Milky Way, signs of the zodiac, comets, meteors, and other astronomical phenomena. 192pp. 8⅜ x 11. 0-486-43981-X

JEWELRY MAKING: Techniques for Metal, Tim McCreight. Easy-to-follow instructions and carefully executed illustrations describe tools and techniques, use of gems and enamels, wire inlay, casting, and other topics. 72 line illustrations and diagrams. 176pp. 8¼ x 10⅞. 0-486-44043-5

MAKING BIRDHOUSES: Easy and Advanced Projects, Gladstone Califf. Easy-to-follow instructions include diagrams for everything from a one-room house for bluebirds to a forty-two-room structure for purple martins. 56 plates; 4 figures. 80pp. 8¾ x 6⅜. 0-486-44183-0

LITTLE BOOK OF LOG CABINS: How to Build and Furnish Them, William S. Wicks. Handy how-to manual, with instructions and illustrations for building cabins in the Adirondack style, fireplaces, stairways, furniture, beamed ceilings, and more. 102 line drawings. 96pp. 8¾ x 6⅜. 0-486-44259-4

THE SEASONS OF AMERICA PAST, Eric Sloane. From "sugaring time" and strawberry picking to Indian summer and fall harvest, a whole year's activities described in charming prose and enhanced with 79 of the author's own illustrations. 160pp. 8¼ x 11. 0-486-44220-9

THE METROPOLIS OF TOMORROW, Hugh Ferriss. Generous, prophetic vision of the metropolis of the future, as perceived in 1929. Powerful illustrations of towering structures, wide avenues, and rooftop parks–all features in many of today's modern cities. 59 illustrations. 144pp. 8¼ x 11. 0-486-43727-2

THE PATH TO ROME, Hilaire Belloc. This 1902 memoir abounds in lively vignettes from a vanished time, recounting a pilgrimage on foot across the Alps and Apennines in order to "see all Europe which the Christian Faith has saved." 77 of the author's original line drawings complement his sparkling prose. 272pp. 5⅜ x 8½. 0-486-44001-X

THE HISTORY OF RASSELAS: Prince of Abissinia, Samuel Johnson. Distinguished English writer attacks eighteenth-century optimism and man's unrealistic estimates of what life has to offer. 112pp. 5⅜ x 8½. 0-486-44094-X

A VOYAGE TO ARCTURUS, David Lindsay. A brilliant flight of pure fancy, where wild creatures crowd the fantastic landscape and demented torturers dominate victims with their bizarre mental powers. 272pp. 5⅜ x 8½. 0-486-44198-9